'What about you? Have you no longing for a husband and children? You are great with children. I see you all the time with other people's children and you are so gentle and patient.'

She turned away from him and Callum knew that he'd fallen into a pit of his own making just as they were getting to know each other on an easier footing. Why had he made the conversation so personal when he knew how much Leonie veered away from such things?

'Yes, I would like a family,' she said eventually, 'but I am wary of those sorts of commitments.'

They were seated next to each other on her sofa. Callum got to his feet and stood looking down on her. He held out his hand and when she took it raised her gently to her feet. They were only inches away from each other, but the look in her eyes made him feel as if it was a million miles that separated them, and suddenly he'd had enough of the tactful approach.

He reached out for her, swept her into his arms and kissed her—gently at first, then with rising passion—until he felt the wetness of tears on her face.

As he looked down on her in dismay she pushed him away.

'Callum, please go. I didn't ask you here for something like this to happen!'

'No, of course you didn't,' he said tightly. 'It won't happen again. You have my promise on that.'

He opened the door, stepped out into the night and was gone.

Dear Reader

If you have read my earlier book, CHRISTMAS MAGIC IN HEATHERDALE, you will be familiar with this charming small market town—and if you haven't here it is in summer time, when a nurse who loves children but has been denied them and a charismatic doctor who has lost his taste for marriage discover the kind of love that lasts for ever.

I do hope that you will enjoy meeting them!

Yours romantically

Abigail Gordon

HEATHERDALE'S SHY NURSE

BY
ABIGAIL GORDON

First published in Great Britain 2014
by Mills & Boon, an imprint of Harlequin (UK) Limited,
Large Print edition 2014
Eton House, 18-24 Paradise Road,
Richmond, Surrey, TW9 1SR

© 2014 Abigail Gordon

ISBN: 978-0-263-23913-3

Harlequin (UK) Limited's policy is to use papers that are natural, renewable and recyclable products and made from wood grown in sustainable forests. The logging and manufacturing processes conform to the legal environmental regulations of the country of origin.

Printed and bound in Great Britain
by CPI Antony Rowe, Chippenham, Wiltshire

Abigail Gordon loves to write about the fascinating combination of medicine and romance from her home in a Cheshire village. She is active in local affairs, and is even called upon to write the script for the annual village pantomime! Her eldest son is a hospital manager, and helps with all her medical research. As part of a close-knit family, she treasures having two of her sons living close by, and the third one not too far away. This also gives her the added pleasure of being able to watch her delightful grandchildren growing up.

Recent titles by Abigail Gordon:

These books are also available in eBook format from www.millsandboon.co.uk

Dedication
For Frances, a very special lady.

CHAPTER ONE

HE WAS HOME, Callum Warrender thought contentedly as he lay watching spring sunshine light up his bedroom in an apartment by a lazy river that ran through the prestigious small market town of Heatherdale. Back where he belonged in the place he loved the best.

After sleeping for most of a long transatlantic flight from America he had woken to hear a member of the cabin staff asking passengers to fasten their seat belts as they would shortly be landing at one of the biggest airports in the area, and, suddenly wide awake, the pleasure of the moment had washed over him.

He'd spent six months on an exchange arrangement with a large children's hospital in the States and for the most part had enjoyed the change and the challenge it had presented. Yet he had refused when the chance to become a regular member of its staff had been presented to him.

Work-wise it hadn't been a joy ride. He'd worked long and hard alongside other experts in his field, with each taking note of the others' expertise in orthopaedic paediatrics. Yet there had been time to socialise too.

He'd been wined and dined by those he'd come to demonstrate his skills to, and had met more than a few attractive women on those occasions who would have liked to get to know him better, but past experience had shown him that the road to romance could be a rocky one.

So could the path up to the moors above the town that he walked with great enjoyment when he got the chance, but unlike that other road there was no heartache waiting for him at the end of it.

* * *

Once he was up and dressed he went to the small convenience store at the end of the riverside and did a food shop. When he returned he prepared his first English breakfast in months and, while enjoying it totally, began to plan his day.

It was Saturday and he wasn't due back at the famous Heatherdale Children's Hospital until Monday. With the day stretching ahead of him, he decided to take that walk up to the moors, the place where he always found the precious peace and tranquillity that his work as an orthopaedic paediatrician sometimes denied him.

He saw himself as a loner who carried past mistakes around with him like a protective shield that no woman was going to break through. Always there were those who tried, but it soon became obvious that he was not in the market for marriage.

And now, with all those thoughts put to the

back of his mind, he had a couple of days to himself. Once out in the open with his pack on his back calm always descended upon him.

Every step took him further along a winding, deserted road that led to higher ground. The magic of the moment was broken when the noise of a motorcycle engine came from somewhere behind him, and in seconds it passed him. It swerved around a bend in the road at a crazy speed then there was the sound of it crashing into rocks at the roadside, followed by startled shouts.

Hurrying to the accident scene, Callum couldn't believe what he was seeing. The motorcyclist lay twisted and motionless beside his vehicle as a group of dumbfounded teenagers looked on, unsure of what to do.

A woman was on her knees beside the injured rider. He couldn't see her face because she was bent over him, trying to loosen his leather jacket to feel for his heartbeat, while at the same time frantically urging the teens to keep calm as some of the girls began to react to the moment with screams and tears.

'I'll take over. I'm a doctor,' he barked.

The kneeling woman had managed to open the injured rider's leather jacket so they could get to his chest and to his relief Callum saw that it was rising and falling. The patient was breathing but without any signs of consciousness.

'Have you got a phone with you?' he asked abruptly, as he noted that both the man's legs were twisted at a worrying angle.

She nodded and reached into her rucksack, but on producing it she shook her head. 'We probably won't get a signal up here.'

'Give it to me,' he said impatiently, 'and if I can't get through, I'll try mine.'

As she obeyed, observing him unsmilingly, he dialled the emergency medical services for the area and surprisingly got a reply.

'We are going to need a helicopter,' he said. 'An ambulance would not be able to get up here. I can give you our exact position as I know the area well. We need help for the injured driver of the motorcycle as soon as possible. Under these circumstances there is little we can do for him other than keep a firm check on his heartbeat and try to ascertain what other injuries he might have sustained in the crash.'

When he handed the phone back to the woman she got to her feet. 'I need to speak to my group. They're very upset by what they've witnessed.'

'May I ask your name?'

'My name is Leonie Mitchell and I'm a nurse,' she said, and saw his surprise. 'I help at the local community centre in Heatherdale in my spare time, along with a friend of mine who is usually in charge of the activities that we arrange for the children, but she isn't well today and I said I would step in so that they wouldn't be disappointed.'

'You can carry on with your walk. There is nothing more you can do here,' he told her. 'It's best if the children get clear of the scene.'

He'd resigned himself to a helicopter trip to a hospital in Manchester. He didn't have to go with the young man, of course. There would be at least one doctor on board when it arrived, but he'd seen the lad's twisted legs and if anybody could put them right, he could.

'And once you get back to Heatherdale can you contact the garage on the riverside? If they can send someone to collect the bike, I will sort out the bill. They can invoice me.'

'I will need an address to do that,' Leonie said, anxiously taking up her kneeling position beside the unconscious rider once more.

Callum didn't answer her; his concern for their patient was increasing.

'He's going into heart failure, we are going to have to resuscitate!' For what seemed like a lifetime, they worked on him together until they could feel his heartbeat once more.

The sound of rotor blades whirring signalled that the helicopter had arrived, and the group grew silent as they watched it land beside them. As the doctor and nurse on board alighted, Callum filled them in.

'We were able to resuscitate a few moments ago as there was no heartbeat, and there are fractures of both legs.'

'Are you a doctor?' the medic asked.

'I'm Callum Warrender,' he replied levelly, and the other man's eyes widened.

'Not the Warrender from Heatherdale Children's Hospital?' he exclaimed as he bent over the injured youth.

'Let's just say that I can spot a fracture a mile off and I'm coming along for the ride,' he replied, and stepped aside as two paramedics appeared with a stretcher.

Oh, no! Not *Callum Warrender*, thought Leonie. Hospital gossip was that he was in America and wouldn't be returning for another couple of weeks, but it would seem that it was wrong. And as she was sister-in-charge of the orthopaedic unit it seemed that they would soon be meeting again. She hoped that he wouldn't recognise her as the same person he'd come across up on the moors, with her hair tucked out of sight beneath the woolly hat that was pulled low down on her head and wearing a shapeless waterproof jacket.

He'd asked who she was and she'd told him her name and that she was a nurse, but he wasn't to know that she was a member of his staff. Callum Warrender had been in America when she'd joined the team.

Once the patient had been lifted on board, with the medics from the hospital in charge, and the pilot was ready for take-off, Callum reminded her, 'Please remember to arrange for the motorcycle to be picked up by the garage beside the river, and tell them the guy from the apartments who fills up his tank there will call in to settle it as soon as he gets back from taking the casualty to A and E.'

With that the doors closed and he was gone. What an awful day it was turning out to be, thought Leonie. First Julie had phoned to say she'd picked up a flu bug and wasn't fit to do the walk. Leonie had been happy to help out her friend, but none of them had been prepared for the shock of witnessing that motorbike accident. It hadn't helped that the rider had been such a young guy. She couldn't blame the kids for reacting as they had.

Callum Warrender's arrival had seemed miraculous. He'd taken charge with brusque authority. That he was used to giving orders had been plain to see, but there was no way was she going to go to a strange garage to ask them to pick up the damaged motorcycle and tell them that someone completely unknown to her would pay the bill. She would settle the account herself.

Her group was getting restless so, putting her concerns for the victim and reservations about the man who had taken charge of the catastrophe to one side, Leonie gathered the group together and they set off on their hike across the moors once again, this time in a less euphoric mood than before.

When they arrived back at the community centre in the early evening Leonie left them to the delights of a disco that had been arranged for them by other helpers and went to find the garage by the river that the brusque doctor had mentioned. After giving them details of where the motorcycle could be found, and paying what appeared to be a standing charge for that kind of thing, she asked them to keep it on the premises until she could find a name and address for the injured rider.

Then returned to her recently purchased yurt, where she rang the hospital that the young man had been flown to.

On being put through to A and E, she explained to a nurse at the other end of the line that she had been present when the accident had taken place, and was informed that the patient had regained consciousness and was in Theatre, having fractures and other injuries dealt with by Mr Callum Warrender from the Heatherdale Children's Hospital, who had travelled with him in the helicopter.

That the young man was being treated and by the best was all that really mattered. There were going to be parents somewhere who would be most thankful that someone like Callum Warrender had appeared out of the blue at the scene of the crash.

The fact that there had also been a highly qualified nurse there as well had paled into insignificance beside *his* presence, she reflected wryly.

Of course, she'd heard a lot about Dr Warrender from her colleagues, like how talented a surgeon he was, but she'd never once pictured in her mind what he would be like. To find that she actually liked the look of him was unsettling, but those moments on the road to the moors would stay in her memory for time to come.

His skin was tanned, his hair dark and he had hazel eyes in a face that had purpose and integrity etched upon it. His physique spoke of strength and stamina and, as with his tan, suggested a rugged way of life. There was no denying he was very good looking yet she hadn't heard any mention of a wife in Callum Warrender's life.

Callum travelled back from Manchester by train. He was tired, and looked forward to grabbing a quick bite to eat at the hotel near his apartment. But first he planned to call in at the community centre to let Leonie know how the patient was progressing.

He was aware that he'd been less than civil out there on the road to the moors and felt an apology was required. The reason for his manner was easy enough for him to understand, but a stranger wasn't going to know how much he cherished time to himself out in the countryside around Heatherdale.

To his surprise he had enjoyed working alongside her to save their patient's life. He also needed to find her to thank her for her excellent and level-headed assistance.

A disco was in full swing when he got there, but there was no sign of the woman he'd come in search of, and when he asked of the middle-aged disc jockey in charge where she might be found he said, 'Leonie has gone home to the yurt. She's had a stressful day from the sound of it. Do you want me to give her a message?'

Callum shook his head. 'No, I need to speak to her personally. Where is it that you say she's gone?'

'She lives on the yurtery on the far side of the river.'

'You mean she lives in a tent?'

'Er, yes, I suppose you could say that,' was the reply. 'Hers is the third one from the entrance to the site.' And with a frown he went on to say, 'I'm not sure if I should be telling you this. I don't know who you are, do I?'

'We were both involved in treating an injured motorcyclist up on the road to the moors earlier on today and I've come to report on his condition, that's all. I'm one of the doctors from Heatherdale Hospital,' he explained, and off he went without further delay as hunger pangs were beginning to make themselves felt.

He'd noticed the development of the latest idea in camping at the other side of the river while he'd been having his breakfast that morning.

It was known by some as 'glamping'. A reference to the attractions of a yurt as against the basics of a tent. He was curious to know how they worked as permanent dwellings.

So when Leonie opened the door of the round, glass-roofed construction to him a short time later his glance went immediately to the décor behind her and he saw that the latest 'must have' for those who wanted something small and cheerful to live in was attractively furnished and quite a lot bigger than it had appeared from the outside. Also it made his solidly expensive furnishings in the apartment seem dull and boring by comparison.

But he wasn't there out of curiosity and was not even sure if he'd got the right place, as the woman observing him anxiously didn't look like the woman of those moments on the hillside. Gone were the woolly hat and shapeless jacket.

She was wearing a pale blue dress with matching sandals, had thick and curling chestnut hair that framed her face damply from recent washing, and was observing him in a way that told him he hadn't come to the wrong place after all.

'Come in,' she invited, and as she stepped back to let him pass asked anxiously, 'So how is our patient now?'

Callum was still in his walking clothes and before he could reply she followed one question with another.

'Have you only just got back?'

He nodded. 'Yes. I operated on him myself, and the news is that he is in Intensive Care at the moment but may be put on to one of the wards in the morning.'

'How serious are his injuries?' she continued.

'Serious enough, but he'll recover,' he told her. 'What about your group? Did you get them safely back to base?'

'Er, yes, no casualties amongst them, I'm pleased to say.'

Leonie was conscious that he was mellower now than he'd been out there on the way to the moors. She'd hardly expected him to seek her out in person to report on the motorcyclist, so why was he here, standing before her awkwardly and making stilted comments?

'I've come to apologise for my abruptness when I came upon you and your group at the scene of what was a nasty accident. My excuse, such as it is, may sound trivial, but I was looking forward to some time on my own in the wide-open spaces after six months of hard grind in the States.

'The thought of having two days to myself before going back to work on Monday morning seemed like precious gold in my busy working life. It isn't often that I get my priorities wrong, but maybe I did this morning, and I'm sorry.'

'When you appeared I felt that you were heaven-sent but could hardly be described as angelic.'

He laughed. 'That is fair comment. I'm known more as a tartar than an angel in my working life.' In reality work was the only life he had these days since his catastrophe of a marriage. 'So, do you accept my apology?'

'Yes, of course,' she replied.

'So what about the bike? Did you have time to call in at the garage to have it collected?'

'They're picking the bike up but won't be sending you the bill. I've paid it.'

He frowned. 'That is not what I asked of you.'

'Maybe, but that is what I've done as I felt that I was partly to blame for not insisting that my group walk in single file. It was because they were all over the road that the young guy on the bike lost control.'

'Even so,' he protested.

'Please don't make an issue of it,' she told him steadily. 'I did what I felt was right and don't want to discuss it any further.'

'All right, so be it,' he agreed. 'Have you eaten since you got back?'

'I haven't yet,' she replied cautiously.

'I was planning to eat at the restaurant at the hotel by the river in a while. If you won't let me pay for the removal of the motorcycle, can I take you for a meal to make up for it?'

'I'm afraid not,' she told him, imagining the gossip that would spring up at the hospital if word got out she'd been seen dining with her boss.

'A friend of mine who works full time at the community centre should have taken the kids on the walk today, but I had to take her place as she'd picked up some sort of a flu virus and sounded quite ill when we spoke this morning. So I need to go round to see how she is and look after her. I will have something to eat while I'm there, but thank you for the invitation.'

'Of course. Maybe we'll meet again some

time and I'll be able to make amends, as I do like to repay my debts.'

'You don't owe me anything, please believe me! It was the least I could do for the poor young guy and compared to what you've done for him it was nothing.'

When Leonie arrived at Julie's studio flat, she found that her friend was feeling much better. She was sitting up and taking notice as Leonie made them a meal and was wide-eyed with astonishment to hear about Callum Warrender's invitation.

'Weren't you the lucky one!' she gasped. 'Was he surprised to know that you are one of the staff on the orthopaedic unit?'

'No, because I didn't tell him,' Leonie told her. 'I said I was a nurse, but either he wasn't interested or in fairness to the man he was too tuned in to the injuries of the motorcyclist to get involved in chit-chat.'

'So on Monday morning all will be revealed between the two of you.'

'Maybe, maybe not,' Leonie said. 'He almost didn't recognise me earlier this evening, out of my walking gear. The uniform might really throw him off track, and anyway, they say that Warrender isn't a woman chaser. That he's had a bad experience that's put him off relationships.'

'In what way?' Julie questioned.

'I don't know any details. I haven't been on the wards all that long. He seems like the kind of doctor who will only see nurses as a pair of hands without their faces registering.

'Anyway, enough about Callum Warrender. How have you been feeling while I've been up on the moors?'

Julie shook her head. 'I do feel a lot better now.'

'Is Brendan coming round later?'

'Yes. We've started making wedding plans. I'd be delighted if you'd agree to be my chief bridesmaid, along with my young sister, if that is all right with you, Leonie. It won't bring back past heartache, will it?'

'No, of course not. The past is the past,' she told her evasively. 'I'm over that and if Brendan is coming to talk about wedding arrangements I'll be off as soon as I've tidied the kitchen. I don't need to tell you not to go to the centre to-morrow. I know what Sundays are like there with every kid in the neighbourhood turning up, but you aren't fully recovered yet.'

'I've already phoned in to say that I won't be there,' she replied, 'so don't worry about me, Leonie, but do let me know what happens on Monday with you know who.'

'I can give you the answer to that now,' she said laughingly. '*Nothing is going to happen. Callum Warrender is not my type.*'

Back at home Leonie felt at a loose end. Julie's reference to the affair she'd had with one of the senior anaesthetists at the London hospital where she'd been employed before coming to Heatherdale had brought back vivid memories of the pain and heartache she'd felt on discovering that he was married. But that had been nothing compared to the raw agony of losing the baby that she'd been expecting.

Since then she'd been wary of any other relationships as the hurt of being deceived in such a way hadn't yet healed; it was still new and agonising. Moving to Heatherdale had been about making a fresh start, but that couldn't erase the memories of the past.

Still, she was genuinely thrilled for Julie and Brendan. They made a strong and devoted couple. However, it was difficult to imagine ever being in that situation herself.

To be asked to be a bridesmaid was a different matter. She was honoured that her friend had asked her and she'd be proud to support her on her big day. She wondered what sort of dress Julie had in mind.

Her reverie was interrupted by the couple from the yurt next door, who were having a few folks round for supper. They asked if she would like to join them. As she accepted the invitation her glance was on the hotel on the opposite side of the river and the memory came back of the one she'd turned down and was now wishing she hadn't.

It would have given her the chance to tell Callum Warrender what she did for a living, instead of him discovering on Monday morning in front of all the ward staff of the orthopaedic unit of Heatherdale Children's Hospital that their acquaintance was not going to be a fleeting thing. Now she still had that doubtful pleasure to come.

Callum sat in the hotel lounge, having a nightcap before returning to his apartment.

He should have been feeling content but he wasn't. The night before he'd been full of the pleasure of being back home and enjoying the weekend ahead, but the day that would soon be over had been full of uncertainties.

The fear that they would lose the boy on the bike when there'd been no heartbeat had been allayed when he and the woman who had been at the scene of the crash had worked on him and he'd begun to breathe again.

That had been followed by him operating on the young man and he'd had no idea what lay ahead regarding that until he'd seen the X-rays, but as usual he'd been in top form and all was going to be well with the lad.

Then when he'd arrived back in Heatherdale he'd sought the Leonie person out to apologise for being bossy and abrupt and, totally out of character, when he'd discovered that she'd paid the garage for the removal of the motorcycle had invited her to dine with him and been refused, which had turned it into a very short reacquaintance.

He'd made a point of telling her why he wanted to take her for a meal and there'd been no finesse in the way he'd done it, so it was small wonder that she'd refused and come up with an excuse that could have been the result of some quick thinking.

Yet, if he was being honest with himself, hadn't he issued the invitation because he'd seen her in different clothes, in a pretty blue dress with her chestnut hair down and the merest hint of make-up, so bringing a moment's brightness to what had been a far from happy day? Or maybe was it because he'd been intrigued by the determination not to be told what to do by him that he'd seen in the green eyes looking into his.

But tomorrow was another day and he was going to let it make up for this one. He finished his drink and headed home. As he glanced towards the bridge that spanned the river between their two residences he heard laughter filtering over on the night air, saw a flash of blue, and wondered what had happened to the sick friend.

When he arrived at the apartment there was an email from his ex-wife, Shelley, to say that she was getting married again to her boss, hoped he would wish her well, and that they were going to live in Australia. He gazed at the screen for a few thoughtful moments and then switched the message off, wondering as he did so why he wasn't surprised.

As Callum walked the length of the corridor that led to the orthopaedic unit on Monday morning his step was light. He was back on his own patch. Back amongst the young patients who came to him for treatment for the long-term or shorter illnesses that were blighting their lives.

It was a place where he'd performed miracles and his staff followed them up with excellent nursing, and nowhere was he happier than there.

The time in America had been rewarding and well spent, but on thinking of the persuasion that had been used to encourage him to join them he only needed to look around him at the familiar sights of Heatherdale Children's Hospital to know that the Americans had never stood a chance.

Here he was and here he was going to stay. He hoped that there wouldn't be any changes in the staff that he had left behind when he'd gone to the States, as they were a well-organised team.

He heard his name called and turned to see his friend Ryan Ferguson, head of the neuro unit, approaching from behind.

'Welcome back, Callum. It's great to have you on board again.'

It's great to *be* back,' Callum told him. 'They wanted me to stay but this is where I belong.'

'Me too,' Ryan agreed, and followed it up by saying, 'Melissa and I are having a belated garden party next Saturday afternoon and we would be really pleased if you could come. You remember how we had our two houses made into one? Well, it's to celebrate that. So how are you fixed? Will you be able to join us?'

He smiled. 'Yes, of course. Since Shelley left for a more interesting life my diary has been empty, just as when she was here it was always full. We never did find a happy medium.'

'Do you ever hear from her?' Ryan asked.

'Yes, as a matter of fact. There was a message from her on Saturday night. She's getting married again, to her boss, and going to live in Australia.

'I don't think there could be two people anywhere as incompatible as we were. I won't make that mistake again, Ryan. Marriage is not for me, but I'm delighted that you and Melissa are so happy,'

Callum checked his watch. 'I'd better get on. I'll see you both on Saturday.'

CHAPTER TWO

LEONIE DIDN'T HAVE a car. She cycled to work
each day through the centre of the beautiful old
market town with its gracious Victorian buildings and famous spa that people came to from
far and wide to take of its healing waters.

Once the town was left behind she pedalled
into open country for a short distance until she
came to the hospital, built from the same local
stone as the rest of the buildings in Heatherdale.

It was Monday morning and she had arrived
earlier than usual with a feeling that was a mix-
ture of expectation and unease. She was worried about Callum's reaction when he realised
that they would be close colleagues.

She'd often heard his name spoken since
coming to join the staff at the hospital as ward

sister in the orthopaedic unit, but had taken little notice as she hadn't known the man. He'd gone to America before she'd started there and therefore was of little interest, but after Saturday's happenings all that had changed. He'd probably think her crazy for not mentioning at some time that she was a nurse at the Heatherdale Children's Hospital, where he was head of Orthopaedics.

Yet there'd been nothing to stop him asking what branch of nursing she was involved in when she'd told him what her occupation was as they'd knelt beside the injured youth, but he'd been too high and mighty to ask such questions and probably wouldn't have been interested if she'd told him, which meant that today he might have cause to regret asking her out in the evening when he'd arrived back from Manchester.

Prodded by a sense of duty, he had sought her out and amazed her by asking her to join him for a meal, an invitation that she'd refused with little graciousness.

Soon, very soon, when she'd fastened her bike up securely and taken off her outdoor clothes, they were going to be in each other's company again, and considering that he'd been in her thoughts ever since Saturday night she supposed she ought to be relieved that the uncomfortable meeting would soon be over and then the less she saw of Callum Warrender the better. Though how she was going to manage that when they'd be required to work closely together, she didn't know.

'Good morning everyone,' Callum announced as he strolled into the two-ward complex that was the hospital's orthopaedic centre. He was greeted by happy voices while Leonie, in a uniform that was a darker blue than the rest, bent over the bed of a fretful toddler and kept her head down.

As his keen gaze swept over those present, Callum asked crisply, 'Where's Janet?'

'She's taken early retirement to look after her mother,' one of the nurses told him with a glance in Leonie's direction.

Well, there was no avoiding it now. Leonie straightened up and looked Callum in the eye.

'I have been appointed ward sister in her place, Dr Warrender. I'm afraid that the opportunity to mention that didn't present itself on Saturday when we met unexpectedly.'

Callum was dumbstruck. She had told him she was a nurse but he'd been too busy running the show to ask anything further. Two surprises on his first morning back he could do without.

Used to working with Janet Fairfax as sister-in-charge, he was sorry he hadn't been there when she'd left. She'd been totally reliable, even though she had family commitments that had kept her on the go. Leonie had a lot to live up to.

He gave a grim smile. He had actually thought

he wasn't likely to meet up with her again. So much for forward thinking.

'Carry on, everyone,' he said briskly He turned to address Leonie directly.

'In a moment, Sister, can you spare a few moments to update me about our current patients?'

She was still soothing the fractious infant but nodded her agreement.

'Then I will see you in my office in ten minutes, Sister…er, I'm afraid I don't know your surname.'

'It is Mitchell,' she said levelly. Returning to her work, she placed the now pacified infant back in his cot and went to speak to parents. They'd been there all night beside their baby, who had been born with a deformation of one of its feet and been operated on the previous day to correct the problem.

All had gone satisfactorily and the relief surgeon who had been filling in for Callum had been pleased with the result of what had been his last task before moving to a Manchester hospital for a spell.

'We are so relieved that our baby's feet are now normal,' the mother said. 'We were going to wait for Dr Warrender to come back, but the chance came and we couldn't let it pass by. We have an older child who was born with the same problem and he operated on her, so it would seem that the fault might be genetic.'

'And if it is, we aren't having any more,' the baby's father said grimly.

When Leonie finished her chat, Callum was at the door of the ward office, waiting for her, and after saying goodbye to the parents she moved towards him and was watched with interest by other staff members.

'Take a seat, please, Sister,' he said, pointing to a nearby chair as she closed the office door behind her. He sat down behind his desk. 'Why on earth didn't you tell me that you were a nurse employed in my unit when we were involved in the catastrophe up on the moors road?'

'It was hardly the moment to start giving you my life history,' she replied. 'I told you I was a nurse to reassure you that I was capable of assisting you, which I did. I wouldn't have expected you to want to know anything else at that moment, and in any case there was nothing to stop you from asking me in which area of nursing I was employed. I came to this hospital a couple of months after you went to America when my predecessor left at short notice because of her mother's health.'

'Where did you work before?'

'At a large hospital in London. This position became vacant just as I'd decided that I needed a change And so I made the move up here.'

'Right,' he said, getting to his feet. 'Now that's cleared up, we'll do a ward round so I can familiarise myself with our patients.'

'Yes, of course,' she said, and led the way to

the first bed, where a ten-year-old boy was engrossed in the tablet that he was holding.

'This is Daniel,' she said. 'He ran across the road when the lights were red, was knocked down by a car and has two broken legs. He is due to go home tomorrow on crutches.'

'So maybe next time he will wait for the green man,' Callum said as he read the notes that were clipped to the end of the bed. When he'd done that he lifted the bed covers to observe heavy bruising in parts that were not covered by a plaster cast. He turned to Leonie. 'I shall want to see X-rays of his fractures, and when he is discharged make sure he's given an early appointment to attend my clinic in Outpatients.'

As they went from bed to bed Leonie described in detail the problems of each young patient and as he listened Callum was aware that Janet Fairfax had been good but she was even better. One thing was very plain to see. Leonie Mitchell was a natural with children, which was more than he had ever been able to say about his ex-wife. Shelley had held no yearnings to bring children into the world, which was something she'd kept quiet about until she'd had his wedding ring on her finger.

It had been the first of many things that they hadn't agreed on as they'd discovered that sexual chemistry alone wasn't enough to make a good marriage.

As they moved from bed to bed it was obvious that Leonie knew exactly what upset each child and, equally, what comforted them, and the only thing that was spoiling his return to base was the fact that he hadn't known that the yurt dweller with the glinting chestnut hair and wide green eyes was a member of his staff. He supposed it should have been a pleasant surprise, but he felt a bit as if he'd been made a fool of.

Their round was interrupted when Callum was paged to attend A and E.

Leonie breathed a sigh of relief as he left the ward, before remembering that she hadn't asked Callum for an update on the young biker they'd treated. She'd make a point of asking him later that day.

It was hours before Callum came back to the ward, looking grimly preoccupied. Leonie hoped that it wasn't anything to do with her appearance in his working life. It seemed that it wasn't. A child had been badly injured when an ancient stone stump in one of the town's parks had fallen over onto her.

'Her name is Carys and she's seven years old,' he told the staff. 'She has a fractured shoulder and two broken arms, which I've dealt with. She will shortly be coming up here to be nursed. Needless to say, she is very weepy and trauma-tised, and being so young doesn't realise that she missed death by inches. Luckily her father saw the stump toppling and pulled her away, but not fast enough to prevent some injuries.' He glanced at Leonie. 'So work your magic on this little girl, please.'

'Yes, of course,' she replied. 'We all will, won't we?'

On his way back from the operating theatre Callum had thought about *his* childlessness in a brief moment of sadness, and pondered, as he'd done many times, how Shelley could be so lacking in maternal feelings. Yet he was aware that it was the woman who inherited the pains and problems of pregnancy and giving birth, and for any who were not prepared to go along that road there had to be understanding.

But in the case of his ex-wife it had been more of not wanting to be bothered with what she called the shackles of motherhood. She had wanted parties and expensive clothes, holidays abroad, what to her was the good life, and when the demands of his calling had sometimes come first and he'd had to refuse, she would go with friends or relations, not prepared to be denied her pleasures.

The marriage had lasted three years, with them growing further apart all the time, and when it had ended with a huge fall-out about that very thing, his only feelings had been of relief and a firm intent to steer clear of marriage in the future.

After telling the ward staff about the injured small girl who'd been hit by the falling stump, Callum went into the office and Leonie followed him to ask about the motorcyclist of two days ago.

'I spoke with his parents last night,' he informed her. 'They wanted to thank us for what we did for their son. He has been moved from Intensive Care and is now in a side ward, so it seems as if he is progressing as I thought he would.'

'How about his mobility and the heart stoppage that we brought him out of?' she asked anxiously.

'His heartbeat is now regular, but regarding any movement, with two fractured legs it will be slow progress, whatever the doctors over there decide to do.

'By the way, I called at the garage on my way here this morning and they'd picked up the motorcycle as soon as you'd been in to ask them to do so.

'When his parents phoned I told them where it was and they've asked the garage to repair it for him. They are insisting on reimbursing you for the money you paid the garage to collect it.'

Before she could reply their patient arrived from Recovery and without further discussion she went to supervise the little girl's transfer to the ward with her traumatised parents by her side.

The day had run its course and the staff of the orthopaedic unit were homeward bound. As Leonie pedalled out of the main gates of the hospital Callum passed her in a smart car and pulled up a few yards ahead.

He wound the window down. 'It's good to have you on the unit, Leonie. You have the right touch with the children and having read your application form from when you applied for the position you also have all the necessary medical knowledge and experience for the position.'

The colour rose in her cheeks and he groaned inwardly at the way he'd sounded so patronising when that was the last thing he'd wanted to be. If he had any doubts as to that was how he'd come across, her reply confirmed it.

'I would have thought that the opinion of the person who interviewed me when I applied for the job would have been enough to reassure you with regard to my abilities,' she said coolly, 'unless, of course, I was proving unsatisfactory.'

'Certainly not that,' he said. 'Surely a word of praise can't be unwelcome?'

'No, of course not,' she said quickly. 'I'm sorry.'

'There's no need to be,' he assured her. He was about to drive off but had one last thing to say that he feared would also not please her.

'You are going to let the biker's parents pay you for having the bike brought to the garage, I hope? If it had been the child of either of us that had been hurt and strangers had shown them such kindness, I think that we would want to do the same, don't you?'

Her reaction surprised him. 'Yes. I suppose so,' she agreed, almost choking on the words, and as she started to pedal away from him he saw tears on her lashes and wondered what that was all about.

Leonie called at Julie's flat on the way home to make sure that she really was over the bug that she'd picked up and found her on the point of returning from a busy day at the community centre looking fully recovered.

They were good friends and noticing Leonie's red-rimmed eyes Julie was concerned. 'Have you been crying?'

Leonie managed a smile. 'Just a moment's blub, that's all.'

'A sick child twisted your heartstrings?'

'Yes, that was it.' No way was she going to go into details about a momentary return to the past. She quickly changed the subject. 'So how are wedding plans progressing?'

'We've decided on a date in June. I'd like to be a June bride, and guess what?'

'Go on, tell me. What?'

'We were going to have the reception at a nice hotel but have had a better offer. The council is having the community centre remodelled and have invited us to have our wedding reception there after a service in the church because we are both staff. What do you think?'

'That would be lovely.' No way was she going to let the mention of weddings and children turn the day into an even more painful occasion.

It was Saturday after what Leonie felt had been a strange week on the unit, getting used to Callum's presence. But she'd adjusted and admitted to herself that, whatever their original meeting had been like, working with him was a pleasure.

To her surprise, the young biker's parents had called at the yurt one evening to repay what they insisted they owed her, and remembering what Callum had said she'd graciously accepted it. They had stayed for a while and had told her over coffee how much they felt indebted to Dr Warrender, who had given of his time and expertise to make sure that their son would walk again without difficulty in the future.

'He spoke very highly of you,' the young guy's mother had said. 'Of the assistance you gave him and of how you had given up your

Saturday to take those kids out into the countryside in place of someone who was sick.'

'And we believe that you also work in the orthopaedic section of the hospital?' his father commented.

'Er, yes, that is so, although Dr Warrender and I have only recently started working together,' she told him, though it seemed like for ever.

That afternoon Leonie took care in getting ready to attend the garden party that Melissa and Ryan Ferguson were having to celebrate the joining of their two houses and, even more delightful, the wonderful entwining of their lives.

She'd got to know Melissa, who was a part-time doctor alongside her husband in the neuro unit of the hospital, when between them they had jointly brought back to health a young patient with a cerebral problem who had spinal problems from a fall. They had been firm friends ever since.

* * *

Callum had spent the morning up on his beloved moors, but had returned before lunch to get ready for the garden party. If the invitation had come from anyone other than Melissa and Ryan he wouldn't be going.

He'd gone to enough parties to last him a lifetime to please Shelley when she'd been around, and ever since the divorce he had toned down his social life until it was almost non-existent, which was going to the other extreme, he told himself sometimes. Today he was going to go through the ritual to please his friends and then would slope off somewhere.

As he parked outside the crescent of elegant town houses where Ryan and Melissa had joined theirs together on the occasion of their marriage, he could hear music and voices coming from the large garden at the back and hoped that his arrival was going to go unnoticed.

Yet he could hardly shuffle in amongst those

there without greeting his host and hostess and presenting their two children with the presents he'd brought them from America. Rhianna and Martha were special and he couldn't help but envy Ryan and Melissa their family.

A taxi pulled up at the kerb edge behind him and when he turned his eyes widened. Leonie Mitchell got out, looking fresh and relaxed in a pretty floral dress that matched her colouring exactly. When she straightened up and saw him standing there her face reddened.

'Hello,' she said uncomfortably. 'I didn't know that you would be here.'

'Ryan and Melissa are friends of mine,' he explained, and as two small voices from not far away called his name, 'and Rhianna and Martha are delightful. They will be here in a moment, eager to see what I've brought them from America. Being around them makes up for a lot of things.'

Leonie didn't know what he meant by that but

maybe she wasn't supposed to. Just as he'd said they would, the two daughters of their hosts came rushing from the garden and threw themselves into his arms.

'So how are my girls?' he said laughingly. 'Ready to see what I've brought you back from America?'

'Yes!' they chorused.

As they delved into the gift bags he'd handed to them he told Leonie, 'I've brought them both mini-cheerleader outfits, complete with pom-poms.'

Leonie observed him in surprise.

He laughed. 'I may not have any kids of my own but I see enough of them to know what to buy them.'

'Yes, I can see that,' she said.

'We'd better go and say hello to our hosts, don't you think?' he suggested.

It looked as if they had come together, and as they followed the two girls to the garden, where there was a good smattering of hospital folk amongst the guests, he said to Ryan, 'Why didn't you tell me that my ward sister was coming so that I could have given her a lift?'

'Sorry about that, Leonie,' Ryan told her, and turning back to Callum said in laughing retaliation, 'Why didn't you warn us that we were going to have to provide loud music all the time for our two cheerleaders?'

As they wandered around the gathering together Leonie was conscious of eyes upon her. She hoped their colleagues weren't speculating too much about them.

The more she saw of Callum the more she was beginning to like him, but past experiences had made her cautious, aware of the hurts that others could dish out to the unwary, and no way was she travelling down that road again.

She knew Callum was divorced. For what reasons she didn't know and didn't want to, but it was pleasant to spend this sort of time with him in an easy atmosphere, away from the hospital, with no strings attached.

To his surprise, Callum found that he was enjoying himself amongst the mixed gathering which was the only kind of socialising he'd involved himself in since Shelley's departure.

Whether the same applied to his companion was another matter.

Leonie had seemed happy enough when they'd first arrived and later when she'd chatted to her friend Melissa, but as time passed he sensed an atmosphere of withdrawal about her that hadn't been there before, and wondered where it was coming from.

The party was due to finish around seven o'clock and he offered to drive her home.

'It's kind of you to offer,' she told him, 'but I don't want to break into your evening. A taxi will be fine, thanks just the same.'

She left the party soon after saying her goodbyes to Melissa and Ryan, and when she looked across at Callum he was on a small putting green with Rhianna and Martha.

He was good with children, both inside and outside the hospital, but hadn't any of his own, as far as she knew, which brought to mind one of the nursing staff saying that his wife had not been motherly-minded.

So they had one thing in common—they'd both been deprived of one of the great joys of life, but under different circumstances. On that bleak thought she left the party and decided to walk home as the sun was still high in the sky.

As she unlocked the door of the yurt Leonie glanced across to the other side of the river to where the luxury apartment complex where Callum lived was bathed in the last rays of the sun. A part of her wished that she'd let him bring her home instead of being so unsociable.

But deep down inside she knew that to refuse had been the right thing to do. Gone were the days when she'd been like putty in the hands of a man, and she was being drawn towards Callum Warrender like he was a magnet as the days went by. It hadn't been that long since she'd been drawn to another man with disastrous results and she was wasn't going to fall into that pit of misery ever again.

Her mouth softened at the memory of Callum's rapport with Rhianna and Martha. He would make some child a loving father one day if he ever married again.

As she slid beneath the bed covers at a time when most of the adult population were setting out to enjoy themselves on a Saturday night, Leonie's last mind picture of the day before sleep claimed her was of Callum playing with Rhianna and Martha at the garden party.

When the party was over Callum drove around the small market town that held so much attraction for so many and faced up to the fact that

Leonie was not yearning for his company, as other women were.

She'd refused his invitation to dinner, taken a dim view of the praise he'd bestowed upon her in the hospital car park, and lastly had turned down his offer to drive her home. There would be no more gestures of friendship on his part. He had no intention of changing what he had vowed to stick with in life after Shelley. He was content in his solitary state and wouldn't have given Leonie a second glance if it hadn't been for the traumatic circumstances of their first meeting.

CHAPTER THREE

As THE DAYS passed Leonie felt that her refusal of a lift home from the garden party had set the pattern for her relationship with Callum away from the hospital. But inside it could not be faulted with each of them extremely aware of the other's dedication to their calling.

Leonie was so incredible with their young patients, Callum thought, both in her efficient nursing of them and insistence that her staff show them the same degree of care. For her own part she was so gentle with the children that he thought if Shelley hadn't had any inclination towards motherhood Leonie Mitchell certainly did. It seemed incredible that she wasn't already married with a family.

If it had been fear that was behind his ex-wife's determination never to have children he could have understood it, but it was the thought of losing her fantastic figure, and what she saw as the ghastly performance of breastfeeding, which he'd pointed out was optional, plus the loss of sleep when it was teething time.

When Easter came and Heatherdale was full of sightseers over the holiday weekend, the magic of the moors and the dales would be pulling him outdoors and Callum had put himself down as on call for emergencies and was hoping he wouldn't be needed.

He'd noted that Leonie's name was top of the staff list for Good Friday. Her social life didn't seem very hectic. He wondered what she did in her spare time.

Reminding himself that he had been shown quite clearly that she was a very private person away from the hospital, he put the concern out of his mind and switched his thoughts to something just as basic but more pleasant—remembering to get Rhianna and Martha the Easter eggs that he always bought at this time.

There was a brass band playing in one of the parks as Leonie cycled home after work at the end of Good Friday, and propping the bike against a nearby hedge she stopped to listen. There were lots of folk about. The café not far away was doing a brisk trade and she realised she was tired and hungry.

Eating there would save having to cook when she got home. She almost walked straight out again, though, when the first thing that registered was Callum and the Ferguson family seated at a table nearby.

Before she could depart they'd seen her. Melissa called for her to join them and there was no way she could refuse. There was an empty seat next to Callum, which she had no choice but to take.

He started the conversation.

'What sort of a day have you had?'

'Busy as usual,' she replied.

'But no emergencies or I would have heard from you,' he commented. 'I had my phone with me all the time.'

Leonie smiled. What was he expecting her to say to that? He didn't have to explain himself. No one worked harder than he did.

A waitress was hovering and when she'd ordered her meal Melissa asked, 'So what have you planned for tonight, Leonie?'

'They're having a disco at the community centre and I said I'd go along to help,' she explained, aware of Callum's nearness.

She wasn't expecting any comment from him. He'd got the message that her life away from the hospital was a private thing, if *life* was the right description of lonely evenings, brightened only by an occasional visit from Julie either going or returning from the centre.

She wondered sometimes why she'd opted to continue her nursing career with children after what had happened to her own baby, but there was comfort in being able to do something for the children of others, as there had been no opportunity to help *her* baby. It had been too late from the start.

When they'd all finished eating they went outside to listen to the band again. Callum hadn't left her side.

'I know you don't like me behaving as if we have any relationship apart from the hospital, but you need have no concerns about that. My life is mapped out how I want it to be and I presume that yours is the same, so do we have an understanding?' he said in a low voice.

She nodded bleakly, thinking that his lifestyle might be from choice, but hers had been thrust upon her, and for evermore she would be wary of giving herself to another man, whoever they might be.

'So how about I come along to that disco too tonight? I can give you a lift there and back to save your legs,' he suggested. 'I've nothing planned for tonight and I'd like to help.'

'Yes, all right,' she agreed weakly, with the thought that he might have *cleared the air*, as he described it, but she hadn't, and wasn't likely to in the near future because it would hurt too much to talk about her past.

Still, Callum had made a kind gesture and she didn't want to make a fuss and draw even more attention to her unhappiness. She bid her farewells to the group and headed back to get ready for the evening ahead.

When Callum pulled up outside the yurt at seven o'clock Leonie was ready and waiting, dressed in jeans and a smart sweater and looking revitalised after a shower.

In spite of their conversation in the park she had taken great care with her appearance. Her hair hung in a bright swathe on her shoulders and her make-up was just right. The last thing she wanted was for Callum to think her dowdy when out of hospital uniform.

She was still in a state of incredulity to think that he was actually prepared to endure the noise and the youthful chatter for a whole evening, and when Julie saw them arrive together she observed them wide-eyed as she went to greet them.

Callum was at his most charming as Leonie introduced them to each other, adding to her friend's amazement, and when Julie told them that they'd been let down by the disc jockey, that he'd got the same bug that she'd had the previous week, Callum offered to fill in.

'I used to do a bit of that kind of thing when I was at medical school. I'll take over if you like.'

And as Julie gratefully accepted the offer Leonie stood beside them in amazed silence.

Julie's fiancé Brendan appeared at that moment and was accordingly introduced, and when told about Callum offering to take on the job of disc jockey thanked him profusely while Leonie wished herself far away. Was this his idea of *clearing the air*? she wondered.

Callum looked at her. If she thought he was going to embarrass her she was mistaken. He'd dealt with the music at discos many a time, and doing it once again would be like the old days before he'd met Shelley and been so besotted with her that he hadn't been able to think straight.

Thankfully he had never let his life with her affect his work in orthopaedics, but it had affected everything else he'd enjoyed, and to be involved with these kids for a few hours, playing music, would be therapeutic.

'You don't need to worry, I won't embarrass you,' he told her with a smile tugging at his mouth. 'What are you going to do while I'm occupied?'

'What I always do on these sorts of occasions, help Julie with the refreshments. Callum, it's good of you to do this,' she said stiltedly. 'You never cease to amaze me.'

Brendan was approaching with the equipment that the disc jockey would need and as Callum watched her walk towards the kitchen he was content for the first time in months with his life away from the hospital, as well as in it.

Whether Leonie was happy in *her* life outside the place he didn't know, but he had his doubts. Sometimes he picked up on a sadness in her and knew instinctively that she wouldn't want to talk about it, but it didn't stop him from wondering what could be its cause.

Later that night, when they arrived outside the yurt beneath a full moon in a velvet sky Callum wondered if he would be invited in for a coffee but no such invitation was forthcoming and he wasn't surprised. Leonie had just a word of thanks for him regarding the transport he'd provided, and in a warmer tone her gratitude for the way he'd saved the occasion by filling the empty DJ spot, and then was ready to go inside, because as far as she was concerned the night was over.

As he drove back to his apartment across the bridge that spanned the river Callum reflected that it would have been a great night back there at the community centre if Leonie had been as easy to communicate with as she was on the wards.

But it was as if she became a different person when away from the hospital. She had been wary and unapproachable in spite of his deliberately casual comment that *his* life was organised and wasn't going to take any side turnings.

If he'd known her friend Julie well enough he might have felt that he could ask tactfully if everything was all right in Leonie's life, but he could hardly ask that sort of question of some-one he'd only just met.

He decided that tomorrow he would let the breezes up on the moors blow away what were probably his imaginings and he stopped off at the hotel for a sandwich and a coffee before calling it a day.

Back in the yurt Leonie was going over the night's events in her mind. Callum was the last person she would ever have imagined rolling up his sleeves and getting involved. He had been a far cry from the man who'd taken over from her up on the moors road, more like the one who had sought her out to apologise for his abrupt-ness.

If she were to be asked which of his attitudes she liked the best it would be when he was on the wards with her. She felt safe then. The hurts of her past were forgotten, and because he'd got one or two of his own, if the hospital grapevine could be relied on, she was more relaxed in his presence.

She'd been totally ungracious when he'd brought her home and had been acutely aware of it, but they'd become closer over the past few hours and she hadn't known how to cope with that. Without saying it outright, Callum had implied a couple of times that he had no intention of being involved in any new relationship, which was fine, but what about her?

She was already attracted to him and the last thing she wanted was another heartbreak after what had happened with her ex. She'd been so naïve and trusting that she hadn't seen it coming.

She'd worked with Adrian Crawley as a nurse. Been captivated by the easy charm that he'd spread around. Aware of the attraction he had for her, Adrian had dated her, and they'd slept together.

When she'd fallen pregnant he had promised

that they would marry when the baby came and she'd believed him. She had been so happy and excited for the future.

Her parents had died in an accident fairly recently and as she was an only child there had been no one to grieve with her and offer comfort. Adrian had brought brightness into her life at a time when she had been at her most vulnerable.

The news that he had a wife living in the north of England had come from the woman herself after he'd confessed his misbehaviour.

In a voice of calm reason she had explained over the phone to Leonie that there would be no husband, no wedding, because Adrian wasn't free and didn't want to be.

When Leonie had tackled him about his horrendous treatment of her, with her first reminder being about the baby she was carrying, he'd had the nerve to suggest that he and his wife would adopt it. She had ended the affair then and there, promising Adrian he'd play no part in their child's life even if they had to fight it out in court.

But it hadn't come to that. Her unborn baby, the only source of joy in a life that had become dark and cheerless again, had been stillborn and it had been then that she'd met Julie, who had been a social worker at the London hospital. They'd become firm friends very quickly and it had been Julie's suggestion that she move up to Heatherdale with her.

With nothing to keep her in London any longer, Leonie had agreed and once there had found herself a position as a ward sister at the famous children's hospital.

She loved it, she loved her job and had been reasonably content until Callum Warrender had appeared in her life, awakening feelings that were too raw and recent to contemplate.

Yet wasn't she fussing about nothing? Callum had told her outright a couple of times that

his life was sorted. It seemed that she wasn't
the only one who'd made a big mistake in the
past, but where he seemed to have accepted his
change of circumstances hers still haunted her
with a sorrow that never went away.

Leonie awoke the next morning to a bright sun
overhead and birdsong in the trees. A fine mist
over the river was gradually disappearing and
as she ate the lazy breakfast that she treated
herself to at weekends her glance was on the
apartments where Callum lived. Suddenly he
appeared in front of the one opposite, dressed
for a day in the great outdoors. She found herself envying him the prospect.

She sighed. It was going to be a long day. Her
home was clean and tidy, any washing had been
laundered and put away, and she couldn't rely
on Julie for company because she and Brendan
needed some time together.

Almost as if they had read her mind a dozen

or so of her neighbours, who had also been tempted by the weather, called round to see if she would like to join them on a walk of their own.

Leonie agreed immediately, quickly packing a picnic and joining the group as they left the site.

'Which route will we take?' she enquired.

'Straight up the road to the moors and along the tops,' she was told. 'Are you up to that sort of thing?'

She smiled. 'I wasn't until a couple of weeks ago when I took the kids from the community centre for a similar walk and had a nasty accident thrown in for good measure, but I am now so no cause for concern.'

Her neighbours were relaxed and friendly and she joined in their chatter as they moved slowly upwards towards the bend in the road where the biker had crashed, but as they drew nearer Leonie became silent as the memory of those moments came back.

As they rounded the bend she gasped in disbelief. Callum was there, looking down at the spot where the two of them had saved a young life. When he saw her his amazement equalled hers.

'Leonie!' he exclaimed, as if there was just the two of them there. 'What brings you out here? You are the last person I would expect to see after what happened!'

'Yes, I know,' she replied, and indicated the now silent group that she was with. 'My friends invited me to join them for a walk on the moors and here I am.'

'So I see,' he commented dryly, and wondered what her answer would have been if he had been the one who'd issued the invitation.

The others were getting fidgety and someone said, 'Do you want us to drop you off here with your friend, Leonie?'

'Er, I'm not sure,' she told them. 'This is the place where Dr Warrender and I were involved in that nasty accident. It has both good and bad memories.' She glanced at Callum's inscrutable expression.

'Maybe it's best if I stay with you folks.' She smiled awkwardly. 'I'll see you at work, Callum.'

'Yes, fine. See you then,' he said with an easy smile, though his smile faded as Leonie moved away. She really couldn't get away from him fast enough!

Since the divorce he'd been very wary of any woman coming on to him after Shelley, but Leonie Mitchell was something else. He need have no concerns about *her*. She would run a mile if he even touched her! So what was it that had made her so much on the defensive?

His day had suddenly turned sour. With a heavy heart he turned and made his way back to his apartment.

He wasn't to know that Leonie was feeling the same. She was ashamed to have expressed a preference to stay with her neighbours when just the sight of Callum made her heart beat faster.

She owed him an explanation and the moment she was back on home ground she would seek him out, explain the reason for her behaviour, and hope that he would understand.

Since moving to Heatherdale she hadn't spent much time in the countryside as there was no one available to explore it with. Julie was always tied up in some way, and the first time she had ventured forth had been on the day that she'd taken the youth group up the road to the moors and met Callum.

So a day with her new friends would have been something to really enjoy if she hadn't found Callum at the very spot where they'd first met, and after letting it appear that she would rather be with them than him she was wallowing in self-inflicted misery.

She returned with the rest of them in the early

evening and the moment she'd said her good-byes, Leonie grabbed her bike, and looking sun kissed and windblown, she set off across the bridge to make her peace with him.

But when she rang the doorbell of the ground-floor apartment that she'd seen him leaving that morning it wasn't Callum who answered. A tall blonde, beautifully made up and dressed in designer clothes, stood in the doorway. When Leonie explained awkwardly that she must have got the wrong address for Callum Warrender the stranger disagreed.

'This is his place, but the sweet guy is showering at this moment, and then he's taking me out to dinner somewhere special. Can I tell him who's called?' she asked in a Texan drawl.

'Er, no,' Leonie told her hurriedly. 'It wasn't anything important. I was just passing.' She jumped back on her bike. 'I hope you enjoy your meal.'

'We always have before,' the woman said, 'but

those times were back in Texas when I played hostess. Tonight Callum is doing the honours.'

Embarrassed, Leonie pedalled over the bridge and into her own small home where she sat in the silence and faced up to fact that the she'd had a narrow escape from making a complete fool of herself.

'What would you have done if I hadn't been here when you arrived, Candace, as I wasn't excepting you?' Callum asked his visitor.

She pouted across at him with rouged lips. 'Guess that's so, but it was meant to be a surprise. I wanted to see you again *and* the hospital that is so important in your life.' She waved vaguely in the direction of the hotel on the riverbank. 'Don't panic, I've booked a suite in that place for the time I'm here.'

'Good,' Callum said, and meant it. Any nearer and she would be inviting herself to stay with him and he was in no mood for that. Candace

Kelsey had attached herself to him whilst he was in America, inviting him to dine at her place several times and latching onto him when he had been working in the same hospital over there. It had been a relief to leave her behind!

But politeness required that he should show her some hospitality in return and as long as she stayed away from him in the hotel he would accept her presence in his life for hopefully not too long.

'How long are you intending to stay, Candace?'

She was an orthopaedic consultant like himself, clever, and beautiful with it, and one of his male colleagues out there had warned that she was on the lookout for husband number two. Candace was making a big mistake if she had him down as a possible candidate. He wasn't harbouring any thoughts about marrying again, *not after Shelley*!

But now she was here, only a short time after

his return, and was no doubt sincere about wanting to see the hospital that meant so much to him.

Yet knowing her, it wouldn't be just *that* she'd crossed the Atlantic for.

He'd suggested taking her out to dinner as she was showing no signs of jet-lag. He was already wondering how much of his time she was going to demand tomorrow.

Then there would be Monday when she'd already informed him she was going to be there, watching him work and taking note of the way the orthopaedic unit was run.

He could cope with her interest in his medical life, he supposed, but wished her miles away with regard to the rest. It was typical of life's twists and turns that after Leonie preferring to stay with her friends when they'd met on the moors road, he'd returned to the apartment to find Candace on his doorstep, panting to renew their acquaintance.

As they drove along the riverbank that branched off onto the main road into the town he cast a brief glance at the group of colourful yurts on the other side and saw no signs of life around the third one in the development, which could mean that Leonie was still somewhere with the folks she'd been with earlier in the day. Was she as wary with any of those guys as she was with him? he wondered.

As Leonie's evening dragged on the silence in the yurt was broken by a phone call from Julie to say that she and Brendan had just seen Callum escorting a glamorous blonde into the most famous of the posh hotels in the town. Did Leonie know?

'Yes, I knew that he was taking a visitor from America for a meal,' she replied listlessly.

'So what's the story?' her friend asked. 'Who is she, Leonie?'

'I truthfully don't know. I called in at his

apartment late this afternoon for a quick word and found her installed there, or so it seemed, and she volunteered the information that Callum was unavailable and sent me on my way. I imagine she is someone he met while he was over there.'

'Well, that's a blow,' her staunch protector said. 'There was I beginning to imagine you with a houseful of little Callums and Leonies.'

'I think not,' Leonie told her, smiling weakly. They chatted for a few more minutes then Julie had to go. In spite of her teasing she understood more than anyone how much Leonie was afraid of putting her trust in another relationship, no matter who the man might be, because Julie had been there for her when her life had fallen apart.

Leonie stayed in all day on Sunday, not wanting to venture into the town or down by the river in case she bumped into Callum and his American friend.

As it happened, she needn't have kept out of sight. Callum had taken Candace to Manchester, which was somewhere she had always wanted to visit, and then, after dining together once more, deposited her safely at her hotel before she could manoeuvre any more time with him.

She had been evasive when he'd asked again how long she intended to stay in Heatherdale, but made it perfectly clear that she was going to spend as much time as possible with him.

He'd groaned inwardly at the prospect as she had already been in touch with the powers that be with regard to her visiting the hospital and had been warmly welcomed.

Why no one had thought to mention her approaching visit to him he didn't know, as he might have vetoed it if he'd known, having seen more than enough of her already. But to the hierarchy there was no problem whatsoever in having a well-known doctor from America amongst them in the role of orthopaedic consultant.

Callum had arranged to pick Candace up at the hotel on his way to the hospital on Monday morning and sighed inwardly. He could imagine the expressions of the staff on the unit when the glamorous doctor turned up.

He was late arriving on the wards with her as he'd had to introduce her to some of the admin folk and then one or two high-flyers had collared them, who had yearnings to do what he'd done regarding his six months in America and, after meeting his companion, were even more keen to transfer over there.

But at last they arrived at the unit and the first person to observe them was Leonie, holding a baby that was howling so lustily his introductions of Candace to the staff were almost inaudible. But he did manage to hear the American doctor say when the two women were introduced, 'But, honey, we've already met, haven't we?'

'Er, yes,' Leonie replied in the silence that had fallen as the little one's cries became a whimper.

'When did you meet?' he wanted to know

'It was shortly after I arrived,' Candace cooed. 'You called at Callum's apartment, didn't you?'

'Yes,' Leonie replied, as she gently placed the baby back into the cot. She wanted to run away and hide. The first blight of the day had been Callum's announcement that the newcomer was going to be with them for a while, and the second, even worse, was the declaration from the stranger that the two of them had met when she had visited Callum's apartment.

Callum had regained his poise. He was silently livid that Leonie should have been embarrassed in such a manner, and turning to the American doctor said smoothly, 'Now that introductions are over, maybe you would like to accompany Sister and myself on the ward rounds?'

As the unit returned to normal he asked Leonie to take over the tour and said, 'My ward sister always has the full details of every child's illness available if I require them. Without her I would be lost.'

Leonie couldn't help but be impressed by the American doctor. Callum seemed to be too as he listened to what Dr Kelsey had to say and in turn came up with his opinions, but Leonie felt that there was a tightness about him, an underlying irritation, and when the two doctors were called to Theatre in the middle of the afternoon the conversation amongst the nursing staff was mainly as to whether he was going to make the glamorous American wife number two.

It was plain to see that Dr Kelsey had designs on him and Leonie thought achingly that this woman would never be the sort of trusting fool that she'd been.

When Callum came back from what had been

a short spell in Theatre, leaving Candace chatting to the staff down there, he said to Leonie in a low voice, 'I'll come over to your place early this evening if that's all right? We need to clear something up.' Desperate to explain the reason for her earlier visit to his apartment, she nodded.

Under other circumstances she would not have wanted him to know she'd been there, as on discovering that he had someone already filling the gap in his life, from the looks of it, she would have let her urge to apologise for being so offhanded every time he wanted to be helpful be forgotten.

Having seen the woman who had opened the door to her, it had become embarrassingly clear that it was just the kind of man he was that made him take an interest in *her* empty life away from the hospital and seek her out sometimes. It had nothing to do with any feelings he might have for her personally. But after that same woman had announced to all and sundry that she'd been to his apartment she needed to explain why.

Callum had suggested calling at Leonie's at seven o'clock as Candace would want him to dine with her again and she liked to eat about eight. He was beginning to wonder how he could see less of her without causing offence, but at the moment he was concerned about two things, the first being that Leonie had been to his apartment and he hadn't known. The very fact of it was worrying because she was so reluctant to have anything to do with him, and the second was to reduce, if possible, the embarrassment she had been caused by Candace announcing the fact in front of their colleagues.

When Leonie opened the door to him she was amazed at the pleasure it gave her to have him in her home, even though it would be briefly.

'Was it true? That you came to the apartment?' he asked immediately.

She nodded.

'Why, Leonie? What did you come for when you don't like to be near me other than on the job?'

'That was why I came,' she said in a low voice. 'It was to apologise for being so difficult when you are so kind to me. Something happened to me once that changed my life and has made me afraid of getting to know anyone too well.'

'I see,' he said softly as light began to dawn. 'Are you going to tell me what it was, so that I understand?'

She shook her head. 'No. I can't. Only Julie knows that and she understands why I'm not able to discuss it.'

He was observing her gravely. 'Fair enough, if that is how you feel. But if ever the time comes when you are ready to share the problem, just let me know, will you? Promise?'

She nodded and he persisted. 'Say it, Leonie.'

'Yes, I promise to tell you if ever I am ready to share my problem.'

He smiled. 'I'm pleased. I'd better go for now. I'm taking Candace to dinner where I'll have to listen to what she thinks of our wonderful hospital. It goes without saying that she won't think it is as good as hers.' He winked good-humouredly. 'See you tomorrow, Leonie.'

In the silence that followed Leonie wished she was able to talk about her past, but they were only just getting to know each other. Their attraction was a frail thing that could be blown away like the petals of a spring flower in a restless breeze if she burdened him with her troubles.

Yet she was happier, having cleared the air between them a little, and when she awoke the next morning to a day that was full of the promise of the time of year *with no petals scattering* she was content for just having been able to talk to him freely for a little while.

When the two of them arrived separately at the hospital later that morning they discovered that a ten-year-old girl had been admitted during the night. She'd fallen down a flight of stairs, injuring her back, when she'd gone to get a drink.

A scan had shown heavy bruising of the spine but no specific bone damage, and the night staff had handed her over to Callum, expecting that he was going to allow her to be discharged with painkillers to relieve the injury, along with advice to her parents to let her rest until the soreness and trauma of the fall had disappeared.

That might have been the case if the child hadn't gone into a convulsive kind of coma as she was about to go home. Callum sent an urgent message to Ryan to join him from Neuro.

Between the two of them they decided that there might be a possible injury to the girl's brain that had been missed. Or perhaps the skull had been fractured? But wouldn't that have showed up on the initial X-rays? Another scan was organised.

The results were surprising. No injuries in the cranium area were found, to the relief of the parents, and by the time their young daughter was returned to the ward she was coming out of what appeared to be an epileptic seizure. It was not good, but it was less worrying than what had been the first concern of the two doctors.

'Was it the fall that triggered it off?' her father asked distractedly.

'We can't say at this moment,' Callum told him. 'We need to do further tests so we're not going to discharge your daughter just yet. The period of unconsciousness could be from the shock of the fall, especially if your child was in darkness when it happened, or a one-off epileptic seizure that she has now come out of safely.'

For once the American doctor had no comment to offer, but Leonie, who was attending to the needs of other young patients along with the rest of her staff, saw that Candace appeared to be listening thoughtfully to what the two men were saying and nodding in agreement.

Or maybe she had gone off track because Ryan had brought his handsome womanising assistant, Julian Tindall, with him. Julian was never one to miss an opportunity to flirt and was already making eye contact with Dr Kelsey.

'Wow!' he remarked to one of the nurses in a low voice. 'If the female staff are all like that over there, I'm going to ask for a transfer!'

The two doctors from Neurology had arranged for the young girl to be transferred to their part of the hospital and as a porter came to collect her, with her parents following, Ryan suggested that Candace might like to see their unit, and after a quick word with Callum she joined them on their way back, well aware of

Julian Tindall's interest and enjoying it thoroughly.

When Leonie and Callum had finished their ward rounds in the middle of the morning he called her into the office.

'How are you today, Sister?'

'Fine, thank you,' she replied, and waited to hear what was coming next.

'That's good,' he said. 'While we have a brief moment together, I have a couple of questions for you.'

He watched her tense and was quick to explain, 'When is the next disco at the centre?'

She smiled. 'I don't know when the next disco is but I can find out, and when I do can I tell them that you're volunteering?'

'Yes. But only if you aren't going to spend the whole time in the kitchen again.'

'OK. It's a deal,' she told him, with the smile still in place.

He laughed. 'I'm not sure if I can cope with such enthusiasm.'

'But what about your other commitments?' she questioned.

'If you mean Candace, I think that lover boy Julian might be about to do me a favour. There was a lot of sexual chemistry around those two earlier.'

'What else did you want to ask?' she enquired warily, concealing her surprise on hearing that the American doctor was not on Callum's list of favourite people.

'As well as being a disc jockey, I am available as a native guide for anyone not having witnessed the full beauty of Heatherdale and its surroundings. Would you like me to give you the tour some time?'

He'd seen her expression when he'd mentioned Julian and his overpowering sexuality and wondered how Leonie would react if he was to comment that the neurologist and Candace would make a good match, and that showing *her* around the countryside would be strictly an exercise in country life as far as *he* was concerned if that was what she was thinking, but he kept silent, not sure if it was true.

Nothing had changed with regard to his desire for a solitary life, but it wasn't ever going to bring him the children that Shelley had denied him, was it? Did he want to spend the rest of his life as a loner?

'How about this coming Saturday?' he prompted. 'The forecast is good for the rest of the week so you should be seeing Heatherdale and the surrounding countryside in all its glory.'

'Yes,' she agreed, much to his surprise. 'I would like that. But only if you'll let me bring a picnic in return.'

'Fine,' he agreed. 'We could always grab dinner afterwards.'

'Er, yes, maybe,' she said, with her smile fading Unwilling to press her further and scare her off again, he didn't push it, just pleased that she had agreed to the walk and picnic.

Callum was in Theatre for the rest of the day, surrounded by medical students as he operated on a small girl with a hip problem that was going to result in her wearing callipers for a short time.

That was followed by surgery on a difficult leg fracture that a young boy had received on the school football pitch.

He'd caught a glimpse of Candace in the hospital gardens with Julian in the lunch hour and noted that the hospital Romeo was a fast worker, but, then, so was Candace. She'd obviously abandoned the idea of pursuing any relationship with himself, thank goodness. She was far too like Shelley.

It was a mellow spring evening and he took a stroll along the riverbank to get a breath of fresh air at the end of his working day. As his glance went to the yurts on the other side he wished that it was only a small iron bridge that separated them instead of both their pasts. Hers seemed to hold something that had hurt so badly that she was wary of all men, or was it just with him that she was on her guard? He wished he knew.

Candace had caught him up at the end of the day and announced she had plans for the evening and he'd tried not to smile. If it had been Leonie that Tindall was bestowing his charms upon he would have been concerned, but the other woman would be a match for Julian any time.

He halted, having seen a glimpse of Leonie on her bike. His spirits rose, but fell again. She was cycling in the opposite direction and he felt as if that was how it was going to be, them travelling along different paths when it came to life outside the hospital. What would it be like on Saturday, he wondered and why wasn't he sticking to his resolve of no involvements?

It was barely daylight on the morning in question when his phone rang and Callum knew that a call at such an early hour was not going to be good news.

It wasn't. When he answered it he was expecting it to be either A and E at the hospital or Leonie's voice on the line, but it was neither. Her friend Julie was ringing on Leonie's behalf to inform him that she wouldn't be able to keep to their arrangements for the day as she didn't feel up to it. Would he accept her apologies?

'What is wrong with Leonie?' he enquired. 'Is she ill? If so, maybe I can help.'

'No, she isn't ill, 'Julie told him. 'She really was looking forward to spending some time with you, Dr. Warrender, but it is the way that things are with her sometimes, I'm afraid.'

'Yes, all right, then,' he said dryly, with the

feeling that whatever the reason Leonie was giving for cancelling their day together it was more a matter of her being wary of him for some reason. Maybe he should just give up with her, it was just that she was such a refreshing change after the Shelley catastrophe.

He wasn't to know that Leonie's past had caught up with her when she'd arrived home from the hospital on Friday evening, and it had brought back all the hurt of the worst time of her life. So much so that there'd been no way she'd felt able to keep her promise to Callum, who was in every way the opposite of Adrian Crawley.

Julie had been waiting for her outside the yurt, looking very serious, when she'd got home and alarm bells had rung. 'What's wrong?' she'd asked getting off the bicycle with all speed.

'Let's go inside first,' her friend had said, and once the door had closed behind them Julie began.

'You won't believe who I saw in Manchester this afternoon.'

'Er, who?' she asked, wondering what all the fuss was about.

'Adrian Crawley.'

Leonie sank down slowly onto the nearest chair.

'Did he recognise you?' she croaked.

'Oh, yes, stopped me to chat about old times, and asked after you.'

'You didn't tell him where I am, did you?'

'Of course not. I loathe that man almost as much as you do because of what he did to you.'

'Was his wife with him?'

'No, they're divorced. He said she never forgave him for his infidelity with you.'

'Why was he in Manchester, Julie?' she asked in tones of dread.

'He said he was there on business but wasn't prepared to say what.'

'Since meeting Callum, I was beginning to

feel that I was putting that nightmare behind me, but it seems I was mistaken,' Leonie had said tearfully. 'So the less I see of Callum out of working hours in the future, the easier it will be. Julie, I can't spend the day with him tomorrow.'

'I don't see why,' Julie had said. 'You were lost and lonely when that monster picked you out and left you pregnant without a second thought.

'Enjoy your day with Dr Warrender and forget all about Adrian Crawley.'

'I can't,' Leonie had sobbed. 'Manchester isn't so far away. I will imagine him lurking behind every bush while I'm with Callum. Please phone him for me in the morning to tell him that I can't make it,' she'd begged, and in the end Julie had obliged, though much against her better judgement.

So much for that, then, Callum thought grimly as he gazed unseeingly out onto what was now a glorious morning. He was going to have to ac-

cept that Leonie was too changeable for someone like him.

Whatever it was that had happened to her in
the past it was clear that she still wasn't over it,
and where he would be only too ready to help
her to face up to her problems, *she* was more
concerned with keeping him at a distance, and
in future that was where he would be, on the
edge of her life, *as if he wasn't there already.*

By the time Monday morning came Leonie
had calmed down, having had the whole of the
weekend to realise that if Adrian did ever appear in her life again, so what? She was a stronger person now. She would be able to cope with
it because she had Callum as a friend and com-
forter. Further than that she daren't think as she
was going to have to face him as soon as she
arrived at the hospital and apologise in person
for cancelling their outing on Saturday.

But she saw that it wasn't going to be as soon as she'd expected.

For one thing Dr Kelsey was very much in evidence and the two of them were already on their way to Theatre when she arrived and didn't resurface until the early afternoon.

When they did Callum merely nodded in her direction and did the ward rounds himself without her assistance, which was unheard of. She was getting the message and could not blame him if he was weary of her changeable moods away from the hospital, but at least he couldn't fault her behaviour on the wards.

Candace had taken herself off to the neurology unit the moment they'd finished in Theatre, and after doing the ward rounds Callum had gone to the staff restaurant for a late lunch. All was quiet amongst their small patients for a moment so Leonie followed him at speed.

She caught him up at the entrance to the canteen and cautiously called his name.

'I just want to say sorry about Saturday,' she told him. 'I don't know what you must think of me, blowing hot and cold all the time, but in truth I'd had some unpleasant news connected with my past and would have been very poor company, Callum.'

'Couldn't you have let me be the judge of that?' he said in a low voice. 'I didn't ask you to spend the day with me because of your entertainment value. I just wanted to show you around Heatherdale and the surrounding countryside, that was all.'

'Yes, I know,' she told him miserably. 'I can understand you being annoyed.'

'I am not so much annoyed as defeated, Leonie. Anyone would think that I wasn't to be trusted, but I've got the message. I shall leave you safe in your ivory tower in the future.'

'No. Please don't do that,' she protested.

'Why not? It's what you want, isn't it?'

'No, it isn't. Look, will you let me make you

a meal some time when you aren't entertaining Dr Kelsey, to make up for standing you up?'

'She is fully occupied with Julian in the neuro unit at the moment,' he said dryly. 'You don't have to make up for Saturday by standing over a hot stove.'

But she was determined to make up for letting him down so insisted. 'When would it be convenient for you to come?'

'Whenever,' he said in a milder tone. 'It's up to you.'

'How about this Friday, when we don't have to get up early the next morning?'

'Yes, if you want,' was the reply, and Leonie flashed him a smile and went back to her duties.

Was he crazy? He was being manipulated by the green-eyed goddess who blew hot and cold whenever the mood took her, but he would go to the yurt on Friday night and see what it was like when she was at home and relaxed with her nightmares put to one side.

* * *

The week passed slowly after their conversation on Monday. In the evenings Leonie tidied her small garden and when that was done turned her attention to the inside of her equally small residence, as if Callum was coming to inspect the place instead of merely sharing a meal.

But she was determined that nothing was going to spoil their time together on Friday evening. She'd been stupid to let a mention of Adrian Crawley get to her like it had, but that was the effect that he'd had on her in the days when he'd left her out in the cold, pregnant and alone, and the revulsion had come back with the memory.

'I'll bring a bottle tonight,' Callum said on Friday morning. 'What would you like?'

'Anything, I don't mind,' she said, smiling up at him.

Was he getting it right with Leonie at last?

She had so many different guises. There was the nurse, cool, confident, and so loving towards the children in their care.

Then there was the yurt dweller, free and content in her bright little cupcake home. Then there was the sad and shy woman who seemed terrified of making any sort of personal connection.

It would be no surprise if he arrived to discover that she wasn't there. Some fool he would look, holding the bottle of wine with one hand and clutching a bouquet of flowers with the other.

He was wrong regarding his surmises. Yes, he was holding the flowers with one hand and the wine with the other, but the woman who greeted him when he arrived at the yurt was warm and welcoming, smiling her pleasure on seeing him, and that was the tone of the evening. They were friends spending time together as they ate the food she'd cooked and drank the wine he'd brought, and as they watched the sun set over the river that separated their two homes Callum asked, 'How long have you lived in this place, Leonie?'

'Do you mean the yurt or Heatherdale?' she questioned.

'Either, both, I suppose. What made you leave the excitement of London for sleepy Heatherdale?'

'I was ready for a change,' she said evasively, 'and when I got to know Julie and she was moving back home into these parts I decided to move to where she was going. That was four months ago and I bought this place almost immediately. How long have you lived here?'

'Twelve years. I'd qualified in paediatric orthopaedics and always wanted to work at the hospital here. I got married three years ago and it was a big mistake. We were totally incompatible, and it ended in divorce.'

'Where did you live during that time?' she asked.

'We had a house at the other side of the town, and when we split we sold it and I bought the apartment, which suffices for my needs more or less.'

'Have you any regrets, Callum?'

'Regarding the marriage or the apartment?'

'The marriage, of course.'

'Not really. I was stupid to marry someone like Shelley. She was a vain social butterfly type. We had no children, which was not my choice, so no kids were hurt by the split. The marriage was a sham.'

He had trodden carefully with regard to Leonie's life and lack of a partner of some kind, but because they were being open with each other he made the mistake of asking about her lack of marital status.

'What about you? Have you no longing for a husband and children? You are great with children. I see you all the time with other people's children and you are so gentle and patient. I imagine that you would be in heaven with a child of your own.'

She turned away from him and Callum knew that he'd fallen into a pit of his own making, just as they were getting to know each other on an easier footing. Why had he made the conversation so personal when he knew how much Leonie veered away from such things?

'Yes, I would like a family,' she said eventually, 'but am wary of those sorts of commitments.'

'I find that hard to believe,' he persisted. 'You're a natural with children,'

'Believe what you like, but it's the truth.'

They were seated next to each other on her sofa. Callum got to his feet and stood looking down at her. He held out his hand and when she took it raised her gently to her feet. They were only inches away from each other but the look in her eyes made him feel as if it was a million miles that separated them, and suddenly he'd had enough of the tactful approach.

He reached out for her, swept her into his arms and kissed her, gently at first then with rising passion, until he felt the wetness of tears on her face, and as he looked down on her in dismay she pushed him away.

'Callum, please go. I didn't ask you here for something like this to happen!'

'No, of course you didn't,' he said tightly. 'It won't happen again, you have my promise on that.' He opened the door, stepped out into the night and was gone.

CHAPTER FOUR

DARKNESS HAD FALLEN and the moon was waning in the sky above as he drove off without looking back. It was in keeping with their diminishing attraction, as that was waning too after his tactlessness of a few moments ago.

He didn't see Leonie at the window, watching him leave, already regretting that the evening had ended on such a sad note. It would be so easy to fall in love with him but if she was still going to let the past rule her life, what chance did the present have.

She had met Callum too soon, before her hurts had been given the chance to heal. It was the wrong time, wrong place, and what had happened to *his* vow to stay free of commitments?

She'd thought him abrupt and bossy when

they'd first met, but working with him, occasionally socialising with him, she had become aware of his true worth and the special kind of charisma that was his alone. She'd begun to wish that the past didn't have such a tight hold on her, but she could never forget the devastation of losing love and her stillborn child.

She waited at the window until she saw the light go on in the apartment across the river and then went slowly to bed with a heavy heart.

The weekend loomed ahead like a black abyss. She went shopping in the small town centre on Saturday morning for the lack of anything else to do and found herself searching for a sign of Callum amongst the busy throng, but in vain. And if she had come across him, what then? There would have been little left to say after the revelations of the night before.

Leonie caught a glimpse of Candace and Julian holding hands in one of the shopping arcades and made a speedy detour. They were the last people she wanted to see.

She called at Julie's place on the way home, desperate to talk to someone who understood, but her timing was all wrong, her friend was full of wedding talk.

About when and where it was to take place, her wedding dress, what the bridesmaids were going to wear, and all the rest of what it took to plan a wedding. Leonie hadn't the heart to burden the bride-to-be with her problems.

After a scrappy lunch she went out again because she couldn't settle inside, and as she was walking through one of the parks that graced the town, Melissa and Ryan were there with the children and called for her to join them.

Melissa was almost eight months pregnant and the four of them were eagerly awaiting the new arrival into their happy family which was so different from the circumstances of her own pregnancy when there had been the pain of how it had come about to cope with, and the grief of her loss.

She was about to make a hasty departure when Ryan mentioned Callum.

'What does Callum think about Romeo finding his Juliet? Or rather the whirlwind romance between Candace and Julian?'

'I don't know,' she told him. 'He hasn't actually said, but if I had to make a guess I would say that he is relieved.'

'Good. He deserves better than her. Melissa and I are so happy that we want to see the same thing for him if possible.'

'Yes, of course,' Leonie agreed weakly. 'But it is up to him, isn't it?'

As she walked slowly back home the thought was there that it might be up to her rather than him if she could let go of the past that haunted her so much. But how to do that when the birth of a child for Melissa and Ryan was going to be an uncomplicated source of joy, while for her it had been anything but that?

Her neighbours phoned just as she arrived back from her meeting with Ryan and Melissa to say that they were all intending to eat out at the hotel on the riverside. Did she want to join them?

'Yes, I do,' she told the caller. 'What time are you meeting?'

'Eight o'clock,' was the reply. 'We'll give you a knock as we go past.' Leonie had agreed to join them not because she was in party mood, far from it, but because Callum sometimes dined there, and she was aching for the sight of him.

She'd put on her blue dress, brushed her hair until it shone and applied make-up with extra care, and chose a necklace of milky pearls to complete the effect of the dress, while telling herself all the time that she was crazy, doing this when Callum might not be there, and even if he was would he notice after last evening's breakdown of communications?

They were twelve in number from the yurts and when they arrived the hotel dining room was half-empty. If Callum had been there she would have seen him immediately, but he wasn't. As disappointment washed over her Leonie asked a member of the bar staff if Dr Warrender had a table reserved and was told that he usually came on the off chance.

As she was settling into the empty seat that her friends had kept for her she heard the barman say, 'Good evening, sir, a lady has just been asking if you were due to dine here this evening.'

'Really?' she heard him comment. 'I can't think who that might be,' and she watched as he went to sit at a table at the far end of the room.

He'd seen her, of course he had. Leonie was

never out of his thoughts, and like turning the knife she was wearing that pretty blue dress of all things, reminding him of how unmovable she could be sometimes.

There was a lot of laughter and high spirits coming from her table and she was joining in. So it would seem that their relationship, if it could be described as that, had been put to rest, filed away, without much heartbreak on her part.

This is crazy, she thought. *I can't manage another cackle. A bucket of tears maybe, but I can't play the part of the merry diner without a care in the world any longer. Callum has seen me, he knows I'm here and isn't even going to say hello. I can't bear it!*

Someone at the table next to him was leaning over to chat and while she was out of Callum's line of vision she told her friends that she had a migraine coming on and would they excuse her? Leaving the hotel, she set off on foot across the bridge.

The sound of footsteps behind made her swivel round. He was there, observing her grimly.

'Are you so keen to avoid me that you left your meal rather than be near me?' he asked. 'You checked with the bartender, didn't you, hoping I wouldn't show up, and now you've rushed out into the night to get away from me without anyone to make sure you arrive home safely. Well, you've got that, whether you like it or not. I'm coming with you right up to your door and no further, so no need to panic.'

'What about *your* meal?' she croaked.

'The same as yours. I've cancelled it.'

'I see.'

'I don't think you do, Leonie. Outside your working life you live in some sort of a cocoon, shut away from all possible hurts, don't you?'

They were almost at her place and when

they reached her door she took out her key and placed it in the lock. She couldn't bear them parting on such a downbeat and hurtful note.

'I asked the bartender if you would be dining there tonight because I needed to see you like I needed to breathe. Not for any other reason, but just to gaze upon you, and it all became too much for me.'

He observed her incredulously.

'The problem is I need time to adjust.' She reached out and touched his face with gentle fingers. 'Thank you for bringing me home, Callum.'

Sunday was a quiet day with each of them looking forward to Monday morning with increased pleasure, but those sorts of feelings disappeared the moment Leonie arrived at the hospital and found Callum grim-faced. Martha, the youngest daughter of Ryan and Melissa, was being brought to A and E by ambulance, having been involved in a car accident on her way to school.

'Some joker came out of a side turning and ran straight into their car,' Callum said. 'She's got leg and arm injuries. Thank goodness I'm here to take over when she arrives. Fortunately Rhianna was going by school bus this morning as her class were going to the swimming baths.'

'Who was driving?' Leonie asked in cold horror.

'Melissa,' was the reply.

'Oh, no! What about the baby and Melissa herself?'

'Melissa has a chest injury from the steering-wheel, and there's a fear shock might send her into spontaneous labour. We don't yet know if she will lose the baby.'

'That must not be allowed to happen,' Leonie cried, with tears streaming down her face. 'It was only on Saturday that I was thinking how fortunate someone in her position was to have a loving family around her during her pregnancy, with no worries or heartache. Ryan will be out of his mind.'

'He's with her now. They are on the way to a Manchester hospital, knowing that I'm here for Martha when she arrives,' he said, and thought Leonie wasn't white with shock, she was grey, in a state of horror, which wasn't surprising, but there had to be something else making her look like that.

At that moment they heard the screech of the ambulance at the side entrance and he was gone, leaving her to start the day's duties with a heavy heart.

When they lifted Martha out of the ambulance she was weeping and frightened until she saw Callum, then she calmed down.

'I'm going to let them take some pictures of your leg and your arm, Martha, and then I'm going to make them stop hurting,' he told her gently.

When the paramedics had lifted her out and were ready to wheel her to the X-ray unit he held her hand all the way and tried not to think about what might be happening to Melissa and the baby.

They met one of the nurses from the unit in the corridor and Callum asked her to send Leonie to him for a moment.

'Are you all right?' he asked when she appeared.

'Yes,' she said in a low voice as she kissed a surprised Martha, who hadn't been expecting to meet someone else she knew. 'Or at least I will be when I know what is happening with Melissa and the baby.' It was there again, an atmosphere of dread that he couldn't fathom. But time was of the essence and he needed to see the X-rays of Martha's injuries as soon as possible.

They could have been worse, he thought thankfully when he saw them. It seemed that she had been sitting in the front seat of the car, farthest away from the impact from the other vehicle, and her arm and leg injuries were simple fractures that would soon heal.

Once he had dealt with them he took Martha to Leonie and her staff to be cared for, and noticed that his ward sister still had the grey look about her, but reasoned that the two women were good friends and it was only natural that she should be so concerned about Melissa and the baby.

Leonie's last words to him from Saturday night hadn't been mentioned by either of them, which was not surprising. She'd hinted that she needed time and he hoped that it was all it was. He was expecting it to be because there had been something different about her during those moments at her door and maybe they might get the chance to talk properly soon, but before anything else he needed to ring Ryan to ask how Melissa was and if there was any news about the baby.

When he rang him his friend's first question was about Martha, and Callum was able to reassure him that he had dealt with two simple fractures that should heal reasonably quickly and that she was fine, being looked after by Leonie and her nurses.

The news on Melissa and the baby was not so reassuring. The baby appeared to be in good health, but there was a concern that a placental abruption could still occur, which might cause Melissa to lose it, and her chest injuries were an added burden to their anxiety over the baby. The medics were debating whether to deliver the baby a month early but the consensus was that if he could remain inside, so much the better.

And then there was Rhianna to worry about. One of the teachers had brought her to the hospital when school was over for the day to be with her sister and she was very weepy and frightened.

'Rhianna can come home with me,' Leonie told Callum as she held her close. 'She'll stay until Melissa and the concerns over the baby have been sorted. I can see her off to school in the mornings and maybe one of the staff could bring her here in the afternoons when it is over, and she can cuddle up to me at night in my bed.'

'I think that would be great,' Callum said, 'except for one thing. It means that all the responsibility is going to be yours, when I should be doing my share. You looked awful when I told you about the baby, which is understandable, but was there any particular reason that I don't know about?'

Leonie looked away, but her voice was steady enough as she told him, 'It was a shock reaction, I suppose. I'm all right now.' She observed Rhianna, who was calming down now that she was sitting beside Martha's bed.

'How long are you going to keep Martha here in the ward?'

'She could go home today if it was possible, but where to?'

'I've got some leave due,' she said. 'If I take it now, I can look after both of the children.'

'How?' he questioned. 'You haven't got the space and have only one bed. Besides, are you sure you're up to it after your earlier upset?'

'That has passed. I can manage all right as long as I get a fold-away bed for myself so that the children can have my double.'

'All right,' he agreed, 'but on one condition, that you let me help in every way possible.'

'Yes, as long as you're happy for me to take some leave.'

'Of course I am. With Ryan in charge at the Manchester end, and you and I running things here, we will at least be taking one burden from him, and in the meantime we keep our fingers crossed for the little unborn one.'

Leonie had paled again, but nodded her agreement.

For now there were arrangements to make regarding settling the children into the yurt.

'I've got a fold-up bed you can use,' he said. 'As soon as our shifts here are over, I'll drive you and the girls to your place, and will do any other chauffeuring that is required. I can take Rhianna to school and bring her back, just as long as I don't have any emergencies to cope with here. If I do, we'll have to have a rethink.'

Rhianna and Martha had always been fascinated with where Leonie lived and both forgot their tears when they were told that they were going to stay there with her until their parents came home.

Rhianna wasn't entirely happy, though. She was still worried.

'Is our baby brother all right, Uncle Callum?'

It was there again on Leonie's face, the expression that he couldn't fathom.

'Yes, as far as we know he is warm and safe and looking forward to meeting his big sisters,' he reassured them. 'For now let's get Martha off this bed and into my car. Then the four of us are going to go to where Leonie lives. There'll be no running around for you, Martha. Back to bed for the rest of the day.'

When he'd driven them to the yurt Callum said, 'I'll come back this evening with the bed, Leonie, and we can discuss how I can be of assistance in any other ways.

'I'll also ring Ryan before I come so that I can tell you the latest news on Melissa and the baby when I get here, and let him know what arrangements we are making for the children. That will be one thing less for him to worry about.

'I've left a message for Candace, asking her to deal with any orthopaedic problems that might arise while I'm helping with the children, which should work out fine as Julian isn't going to have any time for romancing with the responsibility of the neuro unit to cope with during Ryan's absence.

'And Leonie,' he said, with his voice softening, 'nothing in this life is insurmountable when there is someone to share the problem with.

Callum had picked up on her distress every time Melissa and the baby had been mentioned. How long before he put two and two together and made four? Leonie wondered as she watched his car disappear from sight.

But the children were hungry and she put every other thought to one side except for that one and made a meal for the three of them. Once it was over she turned her thoughts to the matter of clothes for them while they were in her care. Access to them was only going to be accomplished if Callum had a key to the Fergusons' home, which was the second question she put to him when he arrived with the bed.

The first was about Melissa and the baby. He reported that Ryan had said that so far everything was under control regarding his unborn son, that Melissa was in a lot of pain with broken ribs, a cracked collar bone and severe bruising, but all she could think about was the baby.

With regard to Leonie's question about a key to the town house where they lived, he confirmed that he did have a spare key that they'd given him for occasions such as the present one, and if she would make a list of everything the children would need he would go and get them straight away.

Callum had eyed Leonie keenly when he'd arrived and wondered what she would be like if it had been a baby of hers that had been put in such a serious situation. Yet her distress wasn't likely to be anything of that nature because as far as he knew she'd never been married.

But there was the fact that he had only known her a short time so was in no position to judge. Some women might have been two or three times married with a few children by the time they were a similar age. But she was too much of a private person to have a past like that, he told himself as he went to get the children's clothes.

When he came back the girls were asleep, with Martha's injured arm and leg positioned away from Rhianna. Callum smiled down at them.

'We have all eaten, but what about you? Have you had the time to have a meal?' Leonie asked him quietly.

'No, but I don't usually eat until later so there's no problem. I'll get something from the hotel.'

'I could put a steak under the grill and do some fresh vegetables with it if you like,' she suggested, not wanting him to go after the awful day that was almost past.

He hesitated. 'Are you sure that you don't want me to go?'

'If you are referring to Friday and Saturday night, no, I don't,' she said softly, and with a glance at the small suitcase she'd given him, 'I can sort the children's clothes out in the morning.'

'All right, then, yes, I would love to accept the offer.' He was smiling across at her. 'And I promise not to ask a single question of any kind or try and kiss you.'

Her colour was rising, the grey look being replaced by a pink flush on her cheeks.

'How would you feel if I asked you about yourself all the time?'

His smile was still there. 'I would love it because I have nothing to hide, and I don't think you have either. You are just a very private person, aren't you?'

'Yes, if you say so, and that is how I intend to stay.'

At that moment Martha gave a little sob in her sleep and Callum went over to where the children were snuggled down in Leonie's bed, took her hand and stroked it gently until she settled again.

Watching him, Leonie ached to tell him about the past that had tarnished her life at a time when she'd had least resistance. But she knew his moral strength and his expectations of those he worked with and socialised with. He was the man who had appeared out of the blue in her life when she'd needed help up on the moors and had been a big part of it ever since.

She hadn't liked him much at first, but that hadn't lasted long. He was everything she would ever want in a man, but she didn't think Callum would see *her* as *his* ideal woman if she ever opened her heart to him about her past.

The phone rang and it was Julie on the line for a chat about the wedding, but when she heard that Callum was there, and was told about what had been happening to Ryan's family she sent her best wishes and rang off.

'Julie and Brendan are getting married soon,' she told Callum. 'She's asked me to be a bridesmaid, along with her younger sister.'

'Sounds nice,' he said, 'and let me guess, they're having the reception at the community centre.'

'Yes, they are, and they want me to bring someone as my guest. Would you be free at all?' she asked, and couldn't believe what she'd said, yet wasn't as taken aback as he was.

Maybe it was because they were involved in a crisis together that Leonie was mellowing, and the barriers would go back up once it was over.

'I would make sure that I was free if that is what you want,' he said casually, 'and I could always do some disc jockeying if they require it as weddings are expensive occasions.'

She was laughing, eyes sparkling at the thought, and told him, 'I'm sure that they will jump at the offer.'

* * *

It had been a traumatic day and the horrors of it were far from over, Leonie thought in more sombre mood as she left Callum to have his meal. There was no way of knowing what tomorrow would bring, but this short time of peace with him was bringing a calm that she was in need of every time she thought about Melissa and the baby, and it was also helping her to see the kiss of Friday night in the right perspective.

Their attraction to each other was increasing by the minute but both had bad memories of the recent past and where Callum's were clear and out in the open, she was still in trauma. If she hadn't been she would have kissed him back with equal passion.

Her thoughts switched to Ryan and Melissa. *Their* lives had been very different before they'd met. Ryan had had no intention of marrying again, like Callum, but for a very different reason. He'd had a deep and abiding love for the wife he had lost, and it had only been when Melissa had appeared in his life that he had found a love just as wonderful as before.

They didn't deserve today's awful happenings. Ryan had lost his first wife in a dreadful accident. His marriage to Melissa was still so new, and the news of their pregnancy had been another healing miracle.

It was a good marriage, the two small girls adored Melissa and she loved them dearly in return. Everything had been wonderful until today.

As if reading her mind, Callum went over to where the children were sleeping and looking down at them said in a low voice, 'I'll ring Ryan first thing tomorrow so that I can tell you what's happening there when I come to take Rhianna to school.'

He was about to leave them and tonight she

wanted Callum to stay for ever, but what good would it do her?

'You know where I am if you need me, Leonie.'

He reached out and held her close for a long moment. 'Fingers crossed for Mum and baby.'

'Yes, oh, yes!' she choked.

After watching Callum drive away, she went back inside to where the children lay sleeping safe in her keeping. If he'd stayed another moment she would have found herself telling him why she was so traumatised by what was happening to Melissa and her child.

When Callum came over the next morning he had better news from Ryan. There were no signs of an abruption and the baby's movements were strong; added to that Melissa was much better, though still in pain from the cracked ribs and bruising of the chest.

'That is wonderful news!' Leonie exclaimed

joyfully. 'No pregnant woman should have to endure the pain of losing the child that she's carrying, but it does happen.'

Callum observed her thoughtfully. 'Could it be that you know someone that it happened to?'

'Yes, but it was quite some time ago,' she said dismissively, and as the children came in from the garden at that moment the subject was closed. Callum involved himself in checking Martha's sling and plaster casts and listening to them describing what it was like, sleeping in the yurt.

When they'd finished he teased, 'I wouldn't mind trying it myself some time.'

'So is that why you brought your bed, Uncle Callum, so we could use it while you had a go?' Rhianna enquired innocently.

'Er, not exactly,' he informed her.

Just then Leonie came in.

'What was all that about?' she asked.

Callum smiled. 'It was just Rhianna sorting

out my sleeping arrangements,' he told her. 'And regarding *arrangements*, I'll pick her up from school too.'

She shook her head. 'No, Callum, we will do that, Martha and I. We have plenty of time to kill and you haven't. We can get a bus or a taxi.'

He sighed. 'All right, whatever you say.' He'd been looking forward to seeing her again when he brought Rhianna home, but had to admit that what she was suggesting made sense, though it didn't stop him from deciding to call in on his way back after he'd seen Rhianna safely into school. It was going to be a long day without Leonie's presence on the unit.

The more he was with her the more she was getting under his skin. It was as if he'd been dead and was alive again, but the past that she never discussed was still an obstacle.

He knew nothing about her parents or any other relatives she might have, and to be fair she knew nothing about his background, but she had only to ask and he would explain how his mother had brought him up single-handedly until she'd met his stepfather, a genial giant of a man from Canada, and had gone to live over there with him.

They kept in touch regularly and he'd known that she hadn't been happy when Shelley hadn't wanted children. Her own life had been hard but she'd never regretted giving birth to him, even after the man who'd made her pregnant had deserted her.

He loved his mother deeply and knew she would adore grandchildren if he ever gave her them, but strangely enough he hadn't mentioned Leonie to her. Probably because it would feel as if he was taking too much for granted as Leonie was still wary of any really close commitment between them.

They had become closer over recent days but not so close that she was ready to talk to him freely about what she wanted out of life, and what if anything life had done to her that she didn't want to talk about.

When he stopped off on his way back he found the two of them feeding the birds on a small grassy area beside the yurt, and when Martha went back inside for more bread he checked how Leonie was doing.

'So, do you feel less traumatised now that we have some good news from Ryan?'

'Oh, yes,' she breathed, 'yes, indeed. As I told you, I knew someone once whose child was stillborn and she was desolate for evermore.'

'Could she not try again?'

'No. It wasn't that sort of situation.'

'Ah, I see,' he said gravely, and would have liked to continue the conversation, but the clock was ticking on relentlessly and he had work to do, so waving to Martha he wished them both a swift goodbye and went on his way.

CHAPTER FIVE

WHEN CALLUM ARRIVED at the hospital Candace was flashing a diamond ring in front of everyone and congratulations were due. Julian had asked her to marry him and she'd accepted after a very short acquaintance, which seemed like no time at all in which to make such an important decision, but they were a pair of chancers and should be well matched.

He had to hand it to the young consultant for creating chaos. If Julian intended going back to America with Candace when her time was up in Heatherdale, Ryan would have to be on the lookout for another second-in-command now that the American doctor had found husband number two. What a contrast, though, to his own relationship with Leonie.

They *were* closer, though far from as close as he wanted them to be, but from now on he was going to pursue the dream of having her in his life, and if she still continued to keep him at a distance there would be some serious questions that he would need answers to.

Leonie phoned during the day to invite him to dinner with her and the children that evening and his spirits lifted. 'Yes,' he told her, 'I would love to. Is there anything you would like me to bring?'

'Just yourself,' she said, 'and if you could get here no later than six o'clock if possible so that the children's meal won't be too near their bedtime?'

'Yes, sure,' he agreed, and hoped that nothing would occur that would make it a promise impossible to keep, as a crisis could appear out of nowhere on the orthopaedic unit, and without Leonie there as back-up when it was over, there would be even more to concern himself about.

* * *

The day was quiet enough in Orthopaedics until the late afternoon when it took on a less calm atmosphere as A and E was suddenly filled with children who had been on a coach trip from their school when the driver had collapsed at the wheel and the vehicle had ended up in a ditch.

Most of them were unhurt but some had sustained fractures and cuts that needed attention, and as the clock climbed up to six Callum took a moment to phone Leonie with the news that he was going to be late, probably an hour or so.

'That's all right,' she told him. 'I will see to Rhianna and Martha being fed and will have my meal with you when you arrive.'

No one knew better than she did the ups and downs of orthopaedics when it came to children, unless it was Callum, and there must have been some cases he wanted to deal with himself or he would have left them to other members of the theatre staff to treat.

It was two hours later, not one, when his car pulled up in front of the yurt. The girls were asleep once more in her bed and the meal was going to be just about edible, but at least Callum was here now.

'So it was worse than you expected?' she said as she met him in the open doorway.

He shrugged wearily. 'It often is, as we both know, don't we? But at least all the young victims are alive and their injuries sorted, and the coach driver is coming round at another hospital from what seems to be a minor stroke. I am sorry to be so late, Leonie, can you forgive me?'

'Of course I can,' she told him softly, and thought she could forgive him anything.

She poured him a drink.

'The food is past its best but is edible if you want to chance it.'

'Of course I want to chance it!' he exclaimed. 'For one thing I'm starving, and for another you have taken the trouble to cook for me again.'

They ate quickly, then went and sat outside so they could talk without disturbing the girls as much.

'I almost forgot, I have news from the hospital that might surprise you,' said Callum suddenly. 'Candace and Julian are engaged. She was wearing a large solitaire diamond ring this morning.'

'Really!' Leonie exclaimed. 'That didn't take long. When and where is the wedding to take place?'

'Here in Heatherdale, some time soon, so I'm told.'

'That will be two weddings on the calendar, then,' she exclaimed. 'Julie's and Brendan's in June, and theirs.'

'Now, how about us making it a threesome?' he teased lightly.

'No!' she said tightly. 'I have no intention of doing any such thing, and if that was a proposal it was insulting.'

'It wasn't meant to be,' he said levelly. 'I just had to find out how little you think of me *and marriage*, and now I know.'

'No, you don't,' she said in a low voice so as not to waken the children. 'You only know what you see, Callum, and it can be misleading.'

The night was turning sour once again, but he had one more thing to say. 'Why can't you let me be the judge of that?'

As he drove away after thanking her for the meal Leonie did nothing to stop him. What was the point? Callum probably thought that she was some sort of drama queen out to make a mystery out of nothing, not aware that his arrival in her life had come too soon.

Melissa and Ryan came home the early evening of the following day and when Callum called by to collect the children he saw that Leonie wasn't showing any signs of accompanying them.

'I expected that you would be coming with

us, as I'm sure Ryan and Melissa will want to thank you for looking after the children.'

They'd been cool with each other when he'd called to take Rhianna to school that morning, but now he was crossing the barriers that they'd put up for each other again and the ache inside her increased.

'I wasn't intending intruding into Melissa and Ryan's first night home,' she told him stiffly.

'Oh, for goodness' sake, Leonie, stop playing the martyr,' he chided. 'I'm not leaving without you, so get in the car.'

Callum was right. She ought to be there to welcome Ryan and Melissa on their return, so she obeyed, with the word 'martyr' hanging in the air. He was wrong about that. 'Fool' was a better word to describe her.

She was being given a second chance of happiness and was too afraid to take it.

There were tears and lots of kisses when Melissa and Ryan held their children close and thanked the two people they had been able to rely on to look after them.

'We nearly lost our little Liam,' Melissa said tearfully, 'but the fates were kind and he's still tucked up inside me, waiting for the big day.'

Callum watched Leonie's expression and it was raw grief that he saw there in spite of the smile she was bestowing upon her friend, and then the moment passed and it was time for the two of them to leave the happily reunited family to themselves.

On the way back to the yurt there was tense silence between them, on his part because every time he said something it was wrong, and on her part because if he touched her, or even looked at her, she would want to collapse into his arms and weep out her misery and the grief she'd bottled up for so long.

She'd called the baby boy that she'd delivered Benedict, Ben for short, and his memory was sacred. It was something she would love to be able to talk to Callum about, but the reason why she'd been pregnant in the first place was why the words would stick in her throat, so she let him drop her off at home after bidding her a curt goodbye.

There was an invitation to Julian and Candace's engagement party behind the door when Callum arrived at the apartment. It was to take place at the riverside hotel on Saturday night. He couldn't think of anything he fancied less, except for the fact that Leonie might be there, but he would wait and see regarding that.

She was back on the unit the following morning now that Rhianna and Martha were home with their parents and Callum overheard one of the nurses ask Leonie if she'd had an invitation to the party.

'Yes,' she replied. 'I can't remember when last

I went to something like that.' That made two of them, then.

His comment to her the other night about theirs making it three weddings had been said as a prod in the direction of their snail's-pace relationship, and also jokingly at the thought of a trio of weddings of such different kinds of people so near each other.

He was going to go to the party on Saturday night for two reasons, firstly because Leonie was going to be there, and secondly because Candace had asked him to walk her down the aisle on her wedding day for lack of any close relation being present. Once married the newlyweds would cross the Atlantic to start a new life together, which would be wedding number one completed.

His position at wedding number two would be less prestigious if his offer to DJ at the reception was accepted, but he knew which wedding he was going to enjoy the most, and as to wedding number three it would seem that it was to be a non-event and it served him right for pushing it.

When Saturday night came he was ready to walk the short distance to the hotel, immaculate in the evening dress requested on the invitation, when the phone rang, and he frowned. It was either going to be Leonie warning him in advance that she wasn't going to the party or an emergency on the unit, and as he lifted the receiver he was hoping that it would be neither.

It was not to be. He was needed at the hospital. The voice on the phone was that of a junior doctor on the night staff who needed his help desperately, and without taking time to change out of his evening wear Callum headed into work. Time with Leonie was denied him, no matter what he did.

Leonie had dressed carefully for tonight's party. She was wearing a long evening dress of pale green silk that set off the red-gold of her hair. Her eyes a brighter green than the dress sparkled with the promise of the night ahead, as she begged silently of the unseen fates that it should not be another let down.

Callum's apartment was in darkness as she passed it, which wasn't surprising as he lived only a short distance away from the party venue, so had probably been one of the first to arrive, and when Leonie stepped into the hotel foyer one of the reception staff pointed her in the direction of the suite where the guests were gathered.

As she shook hands with the engaged couple Julian said, 'So do we take it that Callum has another engagement for tonight? Only he did give us to understand that he would be here.'

'And he isn't?' she exclaimed.

'Er, no,' said Julian. 'He was seen driving in the opposite direction to this place, dressed for socialising somewhere special and wearing all the right clothes for it.'

Disappointment was like a bad taste in Leonie's mouth as she listened to what he had to say. Candace commented that she hoped that Callum's timekeeping and reliability would have been restored to their usual excellence before the wedding, or they might have to bring someone in off the street to walk her down the aisle.

So where was he? His absence had to mean that either he'd heard her say she was attending the party and had gone elsewhere to avoid any more uncomfortable discussions about the two of them, or else had gone living it up somewhere just for the pleasure of it.

Whatever the reason, she hadn't the right to question it. The party was filling up with new arrivals and not wanting to appear rude she decided that she would hang on for a couple of hours and then make a polite exit with some sort of excuse.

In the middle of the evening she was amazed to see Melissa arrive alone, walking slowly and carefully as her bruised state still demanded.

Where was Ryan? It was strange to see her friend arriving without him. She got to her feet and went to greet her.

'How is it that you're alone?'

'I've come for Julian's sake to represent Ryan. He's been called into A and E, along with Callum, and I've left the girls with Mollie, our wonderful housekeeper.'

'Callum is at the hospital!' Leonie exclaimed as her world righted itself. 'Julian doesn't know that. Everyone here thinks that he's giving it a miss as he was seen driving off in the opposite direction.'

'Then they should know better,' Melissa said. 'You can imagine how little Ryan and I want to be separated after what the last few days have been like, but the two men are the same—if there is a child in need they put everything to one side to sort it.'

'Do we know what's wrong?' Leonie asked.

'A young boy who's been sent to Heatherdale from a hospital in Cheshire where they don't have the equipment to deal with the problem of a serious spinal fracture. He broke it in a fall from a tree that he'd been climbing.

'Callum had been hoping that he wouldn't need to disturb Ryan but there was a head injury that didn't look too good. However, Ryan phoned me just a few moments ago to say that has been sorted and he's on his way here, but Callum is going to stay with his young patient for the time being, so I can't see him making the party tonight.'

'No, of course not,' Leonie agreed. 'I'll explain to Julian what is going on back at the hospital and then go to see if I can help in any way.'

Melissa smiled. 'I'm sure that Callum will be pleased to see you.'

As Leonie waited in the hotel foyer for her taxi she wasn't so sure that Callum would be pleased to see her. Their relationship seemed to go up and down like a see-saw, but she was filled with tenderness and regret for imagining him being anywhere else but at the hospital in his absence. It was one of the things she loved about him, his devotion to his occupation, and his clear-cut approach to all the important things of life, and now she was eager to be near him, to let him see that she cared enough to seek him out. The party had been pointless with him not there and when the taxi arrived she was on her way in seconds.

When she arrived at her destination there was just one nurse seated at the desk in the centre of the main ward beneath the subdued lighting that was in use during the night hours.

'I've just heard about the accident and the spinal problems,' Leonie said in a low voice so as not to disturb any of the young patients in various cots and beds dotted about the ward.

'Dr Warrender is still down in Theatre,' she was told. 'He arrived looking a million dollars and within seconds had stripped off and was in his working clothes. Is he expecting you?'

'No, not at all. It is just that we were going to the same party and when he wasn't there everyone was presuming that he was off enjoying himself somewhere else when we should have all known better. I've come to give him moral support and to see if there's anything I can do to help so I'll go and see what is happening down there.'

They were clearing up after the surgery when she went into Theatre. There was no sign of Callum.

One of the nurses said, 'If you're looking for Dr Ferguson, he went a while ago, but Dr

Warrender has gone out into the gardens for some fresh air. It has been a stressful night for all concerned, but he'll tell you all about it himself, I'm sure.'

As she went to find him Leonie sighed. Everyone seemed to know how Callum was going to react when he saw her except her. When she found him in the hospital gardens, gazing up thoughtfully at a star-filled sky, she said his name hesitantly.

He swung round and observed her in amazement. She looked so beautiful in that long green dress and bathed in starlight that it took his breath away.

'What are *you* doing here?' he asked huskily.

'Melissa told me where you were and I came to find you.'

'You left the party because of me!'

'It wasn't a party without you. I was on the point of going home when she arrived and explained what had happened. How bad is it for the boy, Callum?'

'Not good, but better than when he was brought in. The young scamp nearly killed himself. It was no wonder that the junior doctor on night duty was panicking. I asked Ryan to stop by for his opinion about a blow to the head, but a scan showed that there was no bleeding.'

'And are you finished now?'

'Yes, I'd just come out for a breath of air before getting dressed and driving back home. How did you get here?' he asked whimsically, his glance on the dress. 'Not on your bike, I hope?'

She was laughing. 'No. I came by taxi.'

'Do you want to go back to the party?'

'Not particularly, but I think we should as it is your friend who is getting engaged—just as long as you aren't too exhausted after what has been happening here.'

'I'm used to the strains and stresses of this

place,' he said dryly, 'and as long as I can make life happier and healthier for the children who are brought here, I'm fine. I used to dream of having a child of my own to cherish but so far it is the offspring of others that I spend my time with.'

They were back in the hospital corridor beneath bright lighting and he saw that the colour had drained from her face once again. Surely he hadn't said the wrong thing this time?

As he drove them back to the party Leonie was silent. What he'd said had triggered off the feeling of loss that was always there when they talked of anything personal. Their feelings were exactly the same with regard to what he'd said about having a child of one's own but it took two to create a new small being.

The party was almost over when they got there, but for the time that was left Leonie was content just to be by his side, with the future back into the far corners of her mind where it belonged.

She wasn't aware that her leaving the party to seek him out had been responsible for Callum actually seeing that third wedding on the horizon, a long way off maybe, but it was as if church bells were ringing in the distance.

'By the way, have Julie and Brendan accepted my offer to DJ at their wedding?' he enquired.

'Absolutely,' she told him laughingly. 'Julie and Brendan are delighted and wonder if you would mind being called the Disco Doc.'

'I don't mind what they call me as long as the chief bridesmaid is not far away,' he told her, and with his voice deepening, 'I've never met a woman like you before, so beautiful, kind and decent.'

'Don't!' she protested. 'You think you know me, Callum, but you don't.'

'All right,' he soothed, 'so I don't know you, but one day I will.'

She shook her head.

'Oh, yes, I will!' As they were about to seat themselves with their friends he said, 'Big smiles, Leonie. Melissa and Ryan are just recovering from what could have been a tragic loss.'

'I am not likely to forget that!' she told him.

As the four of them chatted Callum worried that he'd lost her again, as the barriers were up once more. Thankfully she didn't stay behind them all the time, but there was always the thought that the day might come when she did.

'I'll take you home once the party is over, Leonie,' he told her, when someone stopped at their table to chat with Ryan and Melissa. 'So don't get any ideas about walking across the bridge on your own if I take my glance off you for a moment, or I'm called away to discuss the wedding with the bridal pair. I have a plus one invite and am hoping that it will be you, so what's the answer?'

It was a moment to let common sense take over, to avoid the chance to be with Callum on a special occasion, but she didn't want to be sensible. It would be an event that she could look back on nostalgically in later years when he'd tired of her evasiveness and found someone else, or gone back to the single life that he'd promised himself.

'Yes, I'd love to be your guest at the wedding,' she told him, 'as long as when it is Julie and Brendan's turn you're still willing to partner me.'

'Of course! Just try and stop me,' he replied, and meant it as he could see Leonie going into her shell at the last moment and all their arrangements falling apart.

As they pulled up at the yurt she made the decision to invite Callum in for a coffee. He must be exhausted after his eventful evening.

He accepted delightedly but said, 'I won't be

able to relax until I've phoned in to the hospital to get an update on my patient.'

'Of course,' agreed Leonie. 'You go ahead while I make the drinks.

He made the phone call. His young patient was stable, which was all he could expect after so short a time, but he would be back there in the morning to check on him before getting involved in any of his weekend pursuits, and as they sat opposite each other, drinking the coffee that Leonie had made, it was as far as he wanted to think about day-to-day matters.

His mind was full of her, the woman in the pale green dress that clung to her curves like a second skin and flared around her ankles at the hemline. He had already made one attempt at marriage and failed, and now, having found the right woman, he couldn't get through to her, so where did they go from here?

At that moment Leonie rose to refill the coffee cups and tripped over the hem of her dress.

As she staggered forward off balance he caught her in his arms and for a brief second she stayed there, looking up at him. He bent and kissed her, gently at first and then a torrent of desire took hold of them.

He began to make love to her, rejoicing at the way that she was responding, until he felt her tense beneath him and then she was pushing him away, desperate to escape his hold, and he knew that nothing had changed.

'I'm sorry,' he said grimly. 'I made the mistake of thinking that we were both in tune with our feelings for once, but it appears not. I would never hurt you, Leonie, in any way whatsoever, but it would seem that now I've got my answer to where we are going together, and it's nowhere.'

Tell him what hurts all the time, a voice in her mind was saying. *You owe it to Callum to be honest with him. It might come over as a some-*

what seedy tale of woe, but it's understanding that you need, not sympathy.

Yet she knew she couldn't do it, couldn't lay bare her innermost feelings when she loved him so much.

'I know you must think I don't know my own mind,' she said wretchedly, 'but you're wrong. I know it only too well. The problem is that as soon as I'm near you everything changes and I forget the promises I've made to myself. I can only think logically when we are apart.'

'Yes, so it would seem,' he agreed dryly, 'and how do you visualise doing that when we are in the same unit at the hospital and live such a short distance away from each other?'

'Moving away perhaps?'

'You would do that to get away from me? Am I so dangerous to be near?'

'Of course not,' she said wearily. 'I'm insane to even think of it, but you don't know the circumstances.'

'And why is that, do you think? It's because you clam up every time we're on our own when I want us to get to know each other better.'

'Yes, I know I do,' she admitted, 'and I also know that every time you come here, except for the one occasion, you leave angry and frustrated, so maybe we should restrict our time together to our hospital commitments.'

'Whatever you say,' he agreed flatly, 'and that being so, I'll see you on Monday morning,'

Leonie felt empty as Callum left, but really what other option did she have?

CHAPTER SIX

JULIE RANG ON Saturday morning to remind her that they were going to the community centre that afternoon to plan out the wedding reception. Talk of the wedding immediately reminded Leonie of Callum. Did their 'plus one' arrangements still stand?

As far as she was concerned, she was committed to be with Callum on both wedding days, she thought as she and Julie discussed the second wedding, which was to be a humbler affair than the first one. But there would be no lack of true love between her friend and Brendan, whereas Candace and Julian Tindall's nuptials would be a lavish affair if she guessed right, but without much else, as the speed with which they were tying the knot was surprising every-one who knew them.

It was ironic that Callum would be one of the central figures on that occasion, while she would be merely an onlooker, and that it would be the opposite on Julie's wedding day when it would be her playing a major part in the pro-ceedings and Callum merely the guest of the bridesmaid until the evening when he would come into his own as the 'Disco Doc'.

If she had any sense she would skip the first wedding and be there for Julie at the second, but leave the reception in the early evening to avoid any more of the futile discussions that al-ways came when she and Callum were together out of working hours. All of which would be simple enough *if she didn't long to be with him all the time.*

It was a warm May Saturday and the throng of visitors and residents of Heatherdale were out to enjoy time spent amongst the small market

town's gracious historic buildings and flower-
filled parks, with a visit included to the pump
room and the nearby well that for centuries had
supplied the famous spa water that many had
turned to, and still did, for health reasons.

A limousine with an open top and decked
with white ribbons was easing its way along
the busy main street to where the parish church
was to be found, and folks were stopping to
stare at the wedding couple who were clearly
on view, which was like manna to the soul of
the bride and bridegroom, who liked to play to
the crowd whenever possible.

Leonie had chosen to sit at the back of the
church to get a clear view of Callum's entrance
with Candace, and when the two of them appeared her heart was filled with thankfulness
that he was not the bridegroom.

She had been the first person he'd looked for
as he'd stood in the doorway of the church with

the bride as they'd waited for the organ to boom forth the appropriate music, and he'd felt gloom descend upon him at the thought of how far away the two of them were from anything like this.

The whole thing was a lavish affair and when the newlyweds had left to catch their flight to the States Callum said, 'All of that was claustrophobic. I need some air, Leonie, what about you? Do you fancy a walk in one of the parks?' He glanced at the hat she was wearing. 'We aren't exactly dressed for the moors.'

She knew the answer to the suggestion ought to be 'no' so why was she saying 'yes'? she wondered crazily as he smiled across at her. They left the splendour of the hotel where the wedding had taken place together, the man with hair dark and crisply waving and hazel eyes that Leonie wished could see into her mind and understand without her having to do the telling of why she was so wary of love.

But the sun was shining, they were together for a short time and she should try and enjoy it.

'So what did you think of the wedding of the year, Leonie?' he asked.

'I thought that it hasn't yet arrived,' she said, smiling across at him. 'There is Julie and Brendan's to look forward to where the Disco Doc will be entertaining people.'

'And a beautiful bridesmaid will be following the bride up the aisle.'

'Er, yes, I hope so,' she said stiltedly. 'I will certainly want to look my best for her.'

They were walking beside the river that ran through a nearby park, the same stretch of water that separated their two homes.

'Dare I ask a question?'

'It depends what it is.'

'Do you have any relatives?'

'No.'

'No parents?'

'No. My father was a pilot and owned a light

aircraft. He took my mother on a flight in what on the face of it was perfect weather, but a horrendous storm blew up from nowhere. He crashed and they were both killed.'

'That is awful!' he exclaimed, resisting the urge to hold her close for comfort. 'And what about brothers and sisters?'

'No.'

'Aunts and uncles?'

'No. My parents were only children and so am I. Tell me about your parents, Callum.'

'My mother is very much alive and well. She lives in Canada, with my father. Well, more accurately he is my stepfather. His name is Brent McAllister and he's a great guy. My actual father is long gone.'

She wasn't sure what he meant by that but didn't ask. It was enough to know that Callum had a loving family in Canada.

It was late afternoon and when they left the park he asked, 'What would you like to do now?'

'I don't know, I haven't given it any consideration,' she told him, taken aback by the question because she hadn't thought any further than the wedding with regard to what the day would hold for the two of them. But it was clear that Callum had other ideas, wasn't expecting them to separate once it was over, and she didn't know how she felt about that.

Over the past few days she'd been congratulating herself on managing to be near him only at the hospital, but the temptation was there and as he waited for a reply she gave in to it and said, 'How about showing me your apartment? When I gaze at it from across the river it always looks so fantastic.'

'I thought you loved the simplicity of the yurt?' he said laughingly. 'And how do you know I won't come on to you once I get you inside?'

'I know because you are special and would

never upset me intentionally,' she said softly, and he groaned.

He could hear himself saying the last time they'd been alone and about to make love to each other that he would never ever want to hurt her and it had been the absolute truth. He would never betray her trust.

'Yes, all right, then,' he agreed, 'and then maybe a leisurely meal that I will cook for us?'

'That would be nice!'

'You haven't tasted my cooking.'

'If it is as excellent as everything else you do, it will be fantastic.'

'Praise indeed!'

'You know that it is so.'

'Not in all things. What about us?'

'Can't we forget that for tonight, Callum, and just be friends?'

He sighed. 'Yes, if you say so,' and looking around him, 'Are we going to walk to the apartment or shall I flag down a taxi?'

'Let's walk, slowly and leisurely,' she said, as he took her hand in his.

'And pretend?'

'Yes, if we have to,' was the reply.

As he showed her around the expensively furnished and immaculate apartment Leonie saw that there was a huge difference in their lifestyles, and wondered how Callum could possibly like the yurt.

There was a big difference between their two homes in more ways than one. They were totally opposite in every way. Yoris the yurt was basic but with a feeling of being lived in, while Callum's apartment was the exact opposite, filled with elegant emptiness.

'So what's the verdict?'

'It is sumptuous,' she replied carefully. 'But it doesn't feel lived in.'

'That's because it isn't. I merely sleep here and have breakfast. The rest of the time I'm elsewhere, mainly at the hospital, and at weekends out in the countryside amongst the hills and dales, unless I'm due in Theatre, as we are both aware that accidents and illness don't just confine themselves to weekdays.'

He was so wonderful, she thought emotionally. It was that which made her draw back into her shell every time Callum wanted their relationship to move on. If only she could see a future for them she would grasp it with both hands, but she was still too shell shocked from past hurts and Callum deserved someone who was ready and willing to be what he wanted her to be.

She wasn't aware that every time he watched her with other people's children on the wards he was amazed to think that he ever contemplated a life without the joys of family life. He wanted her in his life totally, in every part of it.

'What would you like to eat?' he asked, bringing her out of the gloom of her thoughts. 'In spite of my frequent absences from this place

I have a well-stocked fridge and freezer. One of my specialities is roast lamb with fresh vegetables, followed by fruit with clotted cream, and if you are about to say that it would take too long for the meat to defrost, I took it out this morning on the off chance,' he said laughingly, 'though I never expected you'd want to come here in my wildest dreams after the way we left things last time.'

'It was just curiosity,' she made haste to tell him.

'Yes, of course,' he replied smoothly, and thought that to keep telling himself that there was no future for them because of her reticence was pointless. He knew deep down that he would wait for as long as it took for Leonie to let him into the part of her life that she kept under wraps, even if he grew old in the process.

She wanted to help with the meal but he insisted that it was *his* turn to entertain *her*, and as it was a mild night suggested that she make herself comfortable on the balcony of the apartment overlooking the river until the food was cooked.

At peace with herself for a short time, Leonie sat gazing across the water to where the yurt stood pinkly on the other side.

The meal was perfection, as she'd known it would be, and it was when they were having coffee on the balcony at the end of it that her bubble of happiness burst when Callum asked, 'Have Melissa or Ryan been in touch?'

'Not for a week or so,' she replied. 'Why do you ask?'

'They will be doing soon,' he informed her, 'They want us to be godparents to the baby when it arrives.'

'I'm not into that kind of thing,' she told him stiffly.

'What *kind of thing*? It's just a christening we're talking about.'

'Yes, I know but...'

She was out of her depth and uncomfortable, aware that she wouldn't be able to look down at their baby without remembering the stillness of her own.

'If that is the case then you will have to refuse when they ask you, but I will most certainly accept,' he said, observing her thoughtfully, and went on to say, 'You don't have any problems with the infants on the unit—in fact, you are fantastic with them.'

'That is different, it's part of my job,' she told him.

'Yes. OK,' he told her soothingly, 'but, Leonie, be prepared for Melissa and Ryan to be disappointed.'

'They could ask Mollie, their housekeeper. She loves Rhianna and Martha and will be the same with their little brother.'

'No doubt she will,' he agreed, 'but they will want someone younger than she is.'

Leonie got to her feet and reached for the jacket that she'd taken off on arriving at the apartment. Callum wished that he'd never mentioned the christening. Her aversion to the idea didn't fit in with the way she'd looked after Rhianna and Martha at the time of the accident. But they hadn't been newborns.

'Thanks for the meal, Callum, I really enjoyed it,' she said.

He nodded briefly and picked up the car keys as the magic of their time together withered and died, as it always did.

When they arrived at the yurt he didn't get out of the car, just waited until she was safely inside and then drove off.

As dusk turned into darkness Leonie sat hunched in a chair thinking miserably that she needn't have made such a fuss about Callum's casual remark. Melissa and Ryan's baby wasn't born yet. He might be mistaken and they were going to ask someone else to be godmother, and if they did ask her she hoped she would be able to refuse with less paranoia than she'd just displayed.

It would have been so lovely for Callum and her to be the baby's godparents, but the past still had her in its grip and what Callum must have thought of her reaction she shuddered to think.

When he arrived back at the apartment he stayed seated behind the steering-wheel, deep in thought. He'd had no right to question Leonie's comments about the christening. It was *her* life, *her* wishes that she'd been explaining, and if they sounded wrong to him so be it.

One thing was sure, she would have her reasons, and if Leonie didn't want to bring them out into the open that was her choice. He was tempted to go back and tell her that, but as he looked across the river the lights went out in the yurt and he thought that she must be feeling that she'd seen enough of him for one day.

The week that followed was a hectic one, for which Leonie was grateful as it didn't leave much time to think, either on the unit or off it. Quite a few new patients had been admitted with orthopaedic problems that filled the hours of daytime and away from the hospital there was the last-minute bustle of the preparations for the second wedding, Julie and Brendan's, on the coming Saturday.

On Monday morning Callum said briefly, 'What about the disco? I need to know what time it will start so that I can go home to change out of my suit into something less dressy, and also I need to know what sort of music your friends will want me to play for them. Do you know what the average age of the guests is going to be?'

'No, I don't, but can find out,' she replied. 'We're going to the community centre tonight to arrange the tables for the reception, so if you're free it might be a good time to sort out the disco.'

'What time?'

'Half past seven.'

'Do you want a lift?'

'Er, no, I'll go on my bicycle, but thanks for the offer.'

'Sure, any time,' he said levelly, aware that her reaction when he'd mentioned the christening had to be connected with her not wanting to talk about the past, but she surprised him by what she had to say next.

'I would still like you to show me all the parts of Heatherdale that I've never seen,' she told him. 'I've regretted having missed the experience that other time.'

'Really? Well, the offer is still open,' he told her, concealing his surprise. 'Maybe some time after Saturday's wedding perhaps?'

* * *

As the two men arranged the disco that evening
Leonie and Julie chatted as they prepared the
room for Saturday's event.

'How are things between the two of you?'
Julie asked.

'Not good,' was the reply, 'and it's my fault,
Julie. Every time we're getting close I spoil it
with my hang-ups about past nightmares.'

'So next time tell Callum about what happened,' she advised. 'Once it is out in the open
you will know where you stand with him.'

At that moment the two men came to join
them and observing Leonie's expression Callum
guessed that they had been discussing him and
would have liked to know along what lines, but
there was no way he was going to ask.

For the next couple of hours the four of them
concentrated on the wedding preparations and
once that was done made their separate ways
home. Leonie's bridesmaid's dress was in a

large cardboard box on the back seat of Callum's car, as it was too bulky for her to carry while on the bike and he'd offered to drop if off at the yurt.

He arrived before her, needless to say, and rather than risk leaving the dress for her to find he waited until he saw her pedalling over the bridge and when she stopped and propped the bike against the doorpost he passed it to her.

He amazed her by asking out of the blue, 'Have you ever been married?'

He knew it was a strange moment to be asking such a question but having spent the evening helping to get ready for someone else's wedding it was to be expected that marriage was on his mind, and it had occurred to him that Leonie's reluctance to talk about her past could be because of something of that nature, and if it was there was no cause to be embarrassed about it because *he* certainly wasn't with regard to his break-up with Shelley.

'No,' she replied. 'I've never been married *or even had a stable relationship*,' and could have gone on to say, *an unstable one, oh, yes*, but she was tired and miserable, didn't want to have to endure his endless curiosity.

Remembering Julie's advice to tell him about Adrian Crawley and the baby and to be done with the secrecy, she had a sudden longing to pour out her hurt and loneliness of that time and turn to Callum for comfort.

He was observing her expression and said gently, 'You're tired, aren't you? Go and get some rest Leonie. You have a busy weekend ahead.' He glanced at the box she was holding. 'One last question—what colour is the dress?'

'Cream silk. Julie's is traditional white, and the young bridesmaid will be in pink.'

'Sounds great, so why not book a couple of days' leave to relax before the big day?

'It is Julie's "big day", not mine,' she reminded him, with no sign of hers ever materialising, 'and with regard to taking time off I feel that we're too busy on the wards at the moment.'

It was true, but it was also that she wanted to be near him, and the hospital was the only place where they could guarantee being together without the sexual chemistry that came and went so fleetingly that it never got off the ground.

'OK,' he said. 'It isn't *my* wish that you be missing from the unit, it was just a thought, and if that is the case I'll see you tomorrow, so bye for now, Sister Mitchell.'

'Goodnight, Dr Warrender,' she said, smiling across at him, and in that second he took the box with the dress in it from her. She looked at him questioningly as he laid it on the bonnet of the car. He put his arms around her and held her close and covered her face with kisses for the briefest of moments before pushing her away from him gently.

It was then that he saw a single tear rolling

down her cheek. Taking a clean handkerchief from his pocket, he wiped her face gently and when she dredged up a smile told her teasingly, 'It doesn't say much for my kisses if they make you cry. Perhaps it's because I'm out of practice.'

'I wouldn't say that,' she told him, smiling now, and lifting the box with her dress inside off the car bonnet waited to see what he would do next, but much as he didn't want to go he'd seen the tear and until he knew why he kept making her cry he wasn't going to take their attraction any further, so he left Leonie to *her* thoughts and tried to sort *his* out as he drove home, but without much success.

Saturday arrived beneath grey skies in the morning but with the promise of a sunny afternoon for the wedding, and as Leonie helped Julie to get dressed at her flat the only thought in her mind was that everything must be perfect for her friend on her special day.

Unlike the extravagant wedding of the week before, it was on a budget, but there was no shortage of good humour and affection amongst those present when the bride appeared, with her hand resting in the crook of her father's arm and with Leonie and her young sister holding her train.

But one man had eyes only for the chief bridesmaid, who was looking pale but composed in a long cream silk dress, and he groaned inwardly. Would they ever hear wedding bells ringing out for them? He'd thought once that he heard them in the distance, chiming out joyfully on their behalf, but it had just been wishful thinking, his imagination in overdrive.

The disco had been a huge success, with lots of folk wanting to hire him for their functions, but Callum had refused their requests with restrained amusement, explaining that he had another job that was much more important but that if he ever got the sack he would be in touch.

'You are crazy,' Leonie told him laughingly as they waved Julie and Brendan off on their honeymoon, but he didn't respond. *She* was content that she'd managed to keep her yearnings for the kind of happiness that Julie had out of sight until the wedding was over, and was still on a high from the pleasure of knowing that her friend and Brendan had got it right.

But when she saw Callum's expression there was none of the rapport that had been there after wedding number one, when they'd sauntered through the park and she'd asked to see his apartment.

Like all their happy moments there was always the breakdown in communications at some time while they were together that spoilt everything, and now she guessed that he was thinking that where weddings were concerned it was now two down and no signs of the one that mattered most, and as if to confirm that he said, 'I'm ready to go home, Leonie, now the day has run its course. Do you want a lift?'

She wanted more than a lift, she thought bleakly, a lot more. Wanted him to hold her close while she told him what he wanted to know, but it wasn't the right time, not after Julie's lovely wedding. It would wipe out the joy of it.

So she told him, 'I can't leave yet. I need to stay to help tidy up the centre ready for morning, so I'll get a taxi, Callum.'

He was frowning. 'What about your dress?' You shouldn't have to be cleaning in it. Surely you would be better going home to change and then coming back on the bike if you feel the need?'

'The need I feel is to stay here until everything is tidy and *then* go home,' she told him, suddenly feeling weepy and weary because he was being so distant.

'All right,' he agreed. 'Do whatever you think is best. I'll see you on Monday morning, but only briefly. I'm away for the rest of next week. I'm booked to attend a seminar.'

'Who will be filling in for you?' she asked, feeling even more dejected than she was already at the thought of him being absent for almost a week.

'A semi-retired doctor who knows his stuff, so I'm not leaving you all in the lurch. And while on the subject of my being away from the unit, my mother and Brent are coming over soon, so I'll be taking some leave then too.'

'Yes, of course,' she said immediately, wondering what could have happened to the closeness that always came bouncing back after any misunderstanding, but this wasn't like that. She'd enjoyed the day, had no fault to find with it, and thought that Callum had felt the same, but in the last hour he had become a stranger.

Yet she might not feel too content as the night drew in and she was alone with her thoughts of what could be theirs for the asking if she could put the past where it belonged.

She envied him the visit of his family more than words could say and hoped that he would introduce her to his mother when she came, but there was no mention of it and she questioned how her fall from grace could be so sudden.

He couldn't believe he was being so distant, Callum thought as he drove home in sombre mood. He'd been gripped by envy as he'd seen the happiness of today's bridal pair and there'd been frustration too because neither he nor Leonie were committed to anyone else *as far as he knew.*

But she continued to distance herself from him and he'd been hoping that by the time his mother came to visit they would have had a wedding planned and *she* would be there, the one who knew more about pure unselfish love than anyone he had ever met.

But the way things were going, the last of the three weddings was still shrouded in a mist of uncertainty.

CHAPTER SEVEN

MONDAY WAS A drab day, with everything on the wards functioning with normal efficiency but with few sightings of Callum, who was making sure that his replacement for the rest of the week was clued up with what was going on in Orthopaedics.

There was no doing the ward rounds together until late afternoon and then it was the temporary consultant who was by her side as she moved from bed to bed, and it was only as she was leaving the hospital at the end of the day that they came face to face in the car park as Callum was going to his car and Leonie was about to mount her bike.

'Take care,' he said briefly.

'You too,' she replied, and before he'd even

got the car door open she was cycling through the gates and pointing herself and the bike in a different direction from the one he would take. It might be a slightly longer journey but it would let Callum see that she had her pride and wasn't going to beg for his attention.

There was no sign of his return from Manchester, where the seminar was being held, until late on Friday when Leonie saw that the lights were on in his apartment and felt slightly less miserable knowing that he was back where he belonged, whether she saw him over the weekend or not.

But she couldn't help wondering how long he would continue to feel that Heatherdale was where he wanted to be if she was around with her alternately hot and cold, up and down, sad and happy behaviour. She'd thought it before and thought it now—Callum deserved better than that from her and she wasn't able to give it.

* * *

When he'd stopped the car in front of the apartment his thoughts had been running on similar lines and he'd looked across the river to see if the yurt was lit up in the warm dusk, and on seeing that it was he'd smiled.

He wasn't going to take advantage of the fact, but the knowledge that Leonie was near in her little cupcake home, instead of the miles between Heatherdale and Manchester separating them, was better than nothing.

If their relationship hadn't taken a big step backwards he would have been over there immediately, but as far as she was concerned she wasn't expecting him and the hurt of it made her want to weep. Julie had advised that she stop fretting and tell Callum about Crawley and the baby, but she knew that the words would stick in her throat.

If Callum had been someone like Julian, whose morals were shaky to say the least, it wouldn't be so difficult to do that, but the problem would not arise with anyone like Julian because she would never be attracted to someone with his kind of shifting values ever again. Julian and Adrian Crawley were two of a kind.

A knock on the door announced that the honeymooners were back and as she made coffee and they chatted about the wedding Leonie wished that such a happy event hadn't been the cause of the big break-up between Callum and herself.

When Julie asked again how things were between them, not wanting her friend's bubble of happiness to burst, she said, 'We seem to have got it sorted,' and thought that it was true in part but from a different angle. It was over, done and dusted, that kind of sorted.

Leonie went into the town centre the next morning to look around the shops for lack of anything better to do on a Saturday and unbelievably came face to face with Callum on the main shopping street.

It was the kind of meeting from which there was no escape, no side turnings to escape down or supermarkets to get lost in, and she thought miserably that it was incredible that she should even want to do that. Only a short time ago she would have greeted him joyfully and now she was anxious to be gone from him, away from his cool appraisal as she came to a halt opposite him.

'How did the seminar go?'

He shrugged. 'It was all right. Gave me a chance to see the sights of Manchester, I suppose. Any problems on the unit?' he questioned in return.

'No. Everything was fine.' And with no wish to extend the agony, she was about to go on her way.

'Where are you off to?' he wanted to know.

'Nowhere in particular, I'll probably stop for a coffee somewhere and then make tracks.'

'Yes, me too when I've done some shopping,' he agreed. Pointing to the very thing only a few feet away, he said, 'Why don't we try this place for elevenses?'

Not agreeing or refusing, she commented, 'I would have thought you would be up on the moors today?'

'Hmm, I thought about it, but I'm in town to get some things for when my visitors come, such as extra bedding and suchlike. I told you that my mother and stepfather are coming over, didn't I?'

'Yes, you did.'

She was hardly going to forget that as it had been part of his speech when he'd demolished their relationship after they'd waved Julie and Brendan off on their honeymoon, and there was still no mention of introducing her to his relatives when they came, but as their romance was over why should he?

'So are we going to go for a coffee in this place?' he was asking.

'What is the point when we've nothing to say to each other?' she said wearily, and not giving him the chance to reply went on her way.

Callum watched her depart and thought he couldn't blame Leonie for feeling like that after the way he'd behaved after Julie and Brendan's wedding. He'd had a sudden moment of utter frustration that he'd passed on to her and hadn't been much easier to get on with since.

Yet in total contrast he'd bought a ring while in Manchester, a beautiful emerald the colour of her eyes in a fine silver setting that he was longing to put on her finger when they'd sorted their differences, but when was that likely to be, if ever?

So where did they go from here?

* * *

In a coffee shop on the other side of the town Leonie was absently stirring a cup of coffee that had gone cold and wishing she'd been less abrupt when they'd met after the brief separation that had seemed like a lifetime.

She was thinking how wonderful it would have been if she'd met Callum before Adrian. His love would be strong and true, a magical thing that wouldn't falter or betray her. The thought of having him there to hold her in the night, passionate and tender, and in the daytime strong and protective, like a rock in a stormy sea, was making her feel limp with longing.

He wouldn't have taken advantage of her grief and loneliness, but it was done. Adrian Crawley had been there first.

From the way he'd described his mother, Callum's childhood seemed to have been idyllic, with her filling the role perfectly in every way, so his failed marriage must have been hard for her to accept and she was going to be wary of anyone hovering on the sidelines.

If her little Benedict had lived she would have been just as protective of him with regard to *his* happiness in all parts of *his* life, which made it seem all the more important to keep her past to herself, yet how to make her peace with Callum?

As he unloaded the morning's shopping out of the boot of his car Callum remembered Leonie's comment on him not being out in the countryside on such a day, and as it was still some time before midday he decided to change into more suitable clothes and not let the afternoon go to waste. The peace to be found amongst the hills and dales was a precious thing in times of stress or indecision and he was undecided all right!

Common sense said to be patient, give Leonie some space, and maybe soon she would trust him enough to confide in him. But what if she didn't? the voice of reason kept asking. Was he prepared to accept that? He knew that he wasn't.

When he left the apartment with a packed lunch and water to drink in his rucksack, Callum found himself automatically walking towards the place where the accident had taken place and where Leonie and her friends from the yurts had come across him in sombre mood when they had been out for a walk.

It was where the two of them had met and would always stay as clear as crystal in his mind. Whether it had the same appeal for her he didn't know. Probably not as she'd shown no inclination to linger on that occasion and had stayed with her friends during the awkward moment when she'd had to choose between him and them.

What would Leonie be doing now? he wondered as the bend in the road that had been the undoing of the young motorcyclist loomed up in front of him.

He'd heard from the guy's parents a few times and the news had been encouraging as he was mobile again and back on the bike, but taking more care after what had happened.

When he turned the corner Callum stopped in his tracks. It was like history repeating itself but without the trauma of the accident. A group of youths from the community centre was squatting at the side of the road, having a break from the uphill climb, and with them was Leonie, with Julie and Brendan in charge this time. Just to see her standing there was like sunshine after rain.

'It's the Disco Doc!' one of the teenagers cried, and Callum smiled.

'We are just about to eat,' Julie told him, 'and would love to have you join us. Our car is not far away and there's a big hamper in it, which is for the kids to have the chance to celebrate our wedding with us.'

So far Leonie hadn't spoken so he had no idea whether she wanted him to join them or not, but her friend was waiting for an answer and he said easily, 'I'd love to, as long as no one minds?'

She didn't mind, if that was what Callum was hinting at, Leonie thought. After their downbeat meeting of the morning it was a delight to meet up with him again in a happier frame of mind. It was the third time they'd met unexpectedly in the same place, which was strange.

The two previous ones hadn't been happy occasions. This one could be the same if she let it, but Callum didn't deserve that. He didn't have anything on his mind as soul-destroying as she had, and for a short time she was going to forget everything except the pleasure of his unexpected appearance.

They'd moved on a few yards away from the

bend and spread the food out on a grassy area to one side and with lots of soft drinks and a camping kettle steaming away for those who preferred something warmer the atmosphere was happy and light-hearted. If the ward sister and the doctor were struggling with that, no one seemed to notice.

'Did you finish your shopping?' Leonie asked as they sat side by side.

'More or less,' was the brief reply. He wanted to talk about them, not mediocre things such as that, but it was hardly the right moment.

He'd had a phone call from Ryan as he had been about to set out on his walk to say that they were having a few friends round that evening and asking him if he was free to join them. As it was always a pleasure to be with the Ferguson family, he had said that he would and hoped that Leonie might be amongst those that they'd invited.

She was, and sitting beside him in the countryside she was having mixed feelings about the invitation. To be near him would be joy if he hadn't decided to put an end to the overwhelming attraction they had for each other, and then there was the christening.

She hoped that it wouldn't be discussed while she was there in front of Callum. If it was she would have to give a vague answer to what she would have been delighted to agree to under other circumstances and hope that it would be left at that for the time being.

The baby was due any day now and there was always the concern that it might be a safe birth after the accident, with the arrival of a healthy infant for loving parents who had each other to celebrate with.

When all the food had been eaten and the remains of the picnic cleared away, it was time to move onwards and upwards for all those from the community centre, and Callum wondered what Leonie would do now.

Would she leave them to be with him, or do as she'd done the last time in similar circumstances and display no desire for his presence? He soon had his answer.

'Bye for now,' she said, and fell in alongside her friends.

If Callum had asked her to spend the rest of the afternoon with him, she would have done, reflected Leonie. But he'd made it so clear on Julie's wedding day that he was tired of being kept at a distance, that he could play that game too, and now she felt that the easiest way was to go along with it.

When she arrived at Melissa and Ryan's house that evening Callum was there, as she'd known he would be, and it made up a little for the aching feeling of loss when she'd left him on the hillside in the afternoon.

There were a dozen or so folks present for cocktails and canapés, including some of the hospital staff, and amongst them was Julian's replacement, a keen young registrar from the Manchester area who was being introduced to everyone.

Callum was chatting to him when she appeared and smiled briefly in her direction, and then Melissa, hugely pregnant, was by her side with a warm welcome for the friend she wished could be as happy as she was. She knew nothing of Leonie's past, only Julie knew that, but she sensed sorrow and something else that she couldn't quite understand that sometimes came through in her manner.

It was there tonight, so maybe when Leonie was asked to be godmother to their new little one when he arrived it might bring some happiness into her life.

Callum was observing the two of them from the other side of the room and from Melissa's expression guessed the moment that the woman he loved had been dreading had arrived, and he sauntered across to the two of them and said casually to his hostess, 'Can I borrow Leonie for a moment to introduce her to Julian's replacement?'

'Er, yes, of course,' he was told, and as Melissa turned to greet another guest he guided Leonie towards the young registrar and as he did so she said in a low voice, 'You don't forget anything, do you, Callum?'

He smiled a twisted smile. 'If that is the case we have something in common as there is certainly something bugging you etched in your memory for all time, isn't there?'

She didn't answer immediately and he repeated, *'Isn't there?'*

'Yes, there is, and it wouldn't be so difficult to share with you if you weren't so perfect.'

'Perfect! Me? I am far from that. I can be a pain sometimes.'

'Not to me, never to me.'

'So why don't you trust me enough to un-burden yourself of whatever it is that hurts so much?'

She turned away from his searching glance. 'I don't know except that the words won't come when I want to do so.'

He sighed. 'All right, have it your way *for now.* So let's catch the new guy while he's free and I'll introduce you, but I can't keep butting in when you're chatting to Melissa. They have already asked me to be godfather and I've said yes, so now the ball is in your court. If your reluctance is anything to do with not wanting us to be together on that occasion I can't think why *if I'm supposed to be so perfect*!'

For the rest of the evening she was spared having to refuse the invitation that Callum had already accepted because Ryan and Melissa were looking after their guests, and when she was ready to leave at close on midnight her hostess said, 'The next time we meet I have something to ask of you, Leonie.'

She smiled, feigning ignorance.

Callum, who was close by, said, 'I'll get us a taxi, Leonie,' and, when she would have protested, 'You are not going home alone so don't even think of it!'

When they were seated side by side in the vehicle he said, 'So do I take it that you haven't yet been asked to be godmother to the baby?'

She nodded, overcome by his nearness. Her gaze was on his hands, the hands that healed the broken bones of children—other people's children, never his own—and the longing to give him a child was making her weak with the force of it.

The short journey home was over. They were outside the yurt and above them the North Star, which from time immemorial had been trusted by travellers to guide them, was shining silver bright in the night sky and all around them was quietness and the smell of flowers.

It was a night for lovers, Leonie thought achingly, and *she* was in need of guidance, something to point *her* in the right direction regarding her love for Callum. At that moment she felt like throwing caution to the winds, wanting to reach out to him and tell him what he wanted to know, but would she still feel the same when the heat had left her and the longing was under control?

He was observing her questioningly, his dark hazel gaze trying to read her mind, and she told him, 'The magic of the night is getting to me. The silence, the scent of the flowers and...'

Her voice trailed away and he said, 'And what?'

'You here beside me.'

'So I'm not entirely out of favour?'

'You never have been. I wasn't the one who decided to give up on us.'

'But you are the one who doesn't trust me

enough to tell me what it is that made me feel, without knowing the reason why, that I had to rescue you from Melissa when she was about to pop the question about the christening back there.'

She turned away. What he had just said was the unpalatable truth and she didn't blame him for thinking as he did, but it seemed as if *his* life was an open book, while hers was a horror story, and she said over her shoulder, 'Everything you say is true and I am so sorry, Callum.'

'So don't go! Stay here with me and we'll talk about everything except the past.'

She shook her head. 'I can't. The thought of it will still be there like a bad dream.'

He took her arm, swung her round to face him, and with their glances locking said, 'One day you're going to wish you had done me the courtesy of confiding in me.' With that he took his leave, striding across the bridge, his back straight and unbending.

The phone was ringing when Leonie finally went inside. It was Julie on the line, sounding nothing like her usual calm self, as if the news she had to impart had wiped from her mind everything else, otherwise she might have hesitated before telling Leonie of all people that she was pregnant.

'It will mean that we can't afford to buy a house of our own just yet and will have to stay here in this flat for the time being, but we are so thrilled, Leonie.' she said.

'Yes, you must be,' she agreed, 'and I am so happy for you both.' She was, but it didn't stop her pillow being wet with tears as she lay beneath the bed covers.

An hour had passed and sleep was hard to come by. Callum's last terse comment before he'd left her was taking over her mind, filling it with doubts and confusion, as if it wasn't already.

She slipped a jacket on over her nightdress

and went outside to stand in the silence that was only broken by the sound of water skipping over rocks that had been there for centuries in the river bed.

The bridge, only feet away, was well lit for the benefit of those who crossed it at night and she went to stand on it to view Callum's apartment.

It was in darkness and her melancholy increased. It made her feel more shut away from him than ever, but who was to blame for that? Not him.

The sound of young voices broke into her thoughts, shouts of glee and laughter coming from the river below, and when she looked down she saw two teenage boys were trying to steer a homemade raft that looked a lot less than safe in the direction of where the hotel stood on the river bank beside a weir. There was a drop at the other side that would take them into deep water littered with rocks.

'Boys. You must turn back, it isn't safe!' she

cried, leaning over the rail of the bridge, but they just waved the frying pans that they were using as oars and sailed on.

In a flash Leonie was off the bridge and running along the path beside the river, trying to catch up with them and shouting all the time for them to turn back, but it was too late. The current was much stronger as it flowed nearer to the weir and the flimsy raft was totally out of their control as it went over the drop on the other side.

As she finally drew level there was the sight of the wreckage floating on top of the water and one of the boys, face down and unmoving, being swept along into deeper water while the other one was struggling to get to the bank.

After flinging off her jacket, she bent and tied a large knot in the hem of her nightdress to stop it from ballooning around her and prepared to jump in as the other lad reached the safety of the bank.

'Midge is going to drown, isn't he?' he cried hysterically.

'Not if I can help it,' she told him grimly.

'There's a guy!' he cried, pointing towards the opposite bank, but Leonie didn't hear him. She was already swimming towards his injured friend.

Instead of going straight to the apartment when he'd left Leonie, Callum had gone to the hotel and had lingered, with no wish to be alone with his thoughts, until at last he had reluctantly left for the short walk back that took him past the weir.

He was stopped in his tracks by a frightened young voice calling to him from the other side, telling him that a lady had gone into the river to try to rescue his friend, that they'd been on a raft and she'd been on the bridge. Callum was already half out of his jacket and kicking off his shoes.

'All right, stay there!' he bellowed as he threw himself into the water, 'and if you've got a phone that isn't waterlogged, call for an ambulance!'

He consoled himself at the same time with the thought that Leonie would be long asleep, so the head he could see bobbing up and down way ahead of him wouldn't be hers, would it?

She had reached the boy and was trying to turn him over as she made for the bank but he was a dead weight and not a slim kid by any means, and when a voice spoke from behind her she almost let the lad go in the shock of it because it was Callum's voice!

'I'll take over, Leonie. You make for the bank. What on earth are you doing here at this hour?' Are you trying to give me a heart attack?'

She obeyed him, just as amazed as he was, and when he brought the lad to the bank and the two of them began to work on him desperately it seemed like that other time when it had

been the motorcyclist that had brought them together unexpectedly.

It was like an eternity before the boy began to
cough up river water and opened his eyes, and
they exchanged damp smiles above his head,
which was bloodied as if he had hit a rock or
some similar object as he'd fallen off the raft.

Leonie was beginning to shiver and Callum
wished he had something warm and dry to wrap
around her, deciding that when this was sorted
he was going to take her back to his place.

At that moment they heard the siren of a fast-
approaching ambulance and he thought thankfully that the other kid must have found his
phone useable. He knew she would want him to
see to the injured teenager before anything else,
but they were both soaking wet and he wanted
no harm to come to her.

When the paramedics had carried their young
patient carefully on board the ambulance, covered with blankets, and had provided Leonie

with one to wrap around herself, they picked up his friend from the opposite bank and did the same for him.

When that was done Callum told them to take the two boys to the children's hospital with all speed, that he would follow on after getting cleaned up and into some dry clothes, and that in the meantime he would get in touch with Ryan, who was in charge of Neurology, and ask him to go there as soon as possible as the boy had lapsed into unconsciousness again and there was a deep gash on his head.

Leonie was blue with cold in a soaking wet nightdress in what were the chilliest hours of the night, but she would have protested at them not accompanying the young rafter all the way to the hospital. Callum, reading her mind, said, 'It is the sensible thing to do, us going to get dry and into fresh clothes, and then I'll follow the ambulance without delay.'

She nodded. He was right, of course, though

she would rather have gone straight to the yurt to get cleaned up and into some dry clothes instead of his apartment. But once again they'd been a team, the two of them working together for the good of others but never getting any closer to each other,

Just thinking about what had happened to her brought a bitter taste to her mouth that had nothing to do with any river water she might have swallowed. It was because of the tricks that fate had played on her by letting her meet Adrian Crawley and be seduced by him when there were men like Callum in the world.

She often thought that to be able to have *his* children would be joy unspeakable and as she didn't want to keep them any further apart by refusing to go to his place she said, 'I hope that you're going to be able to find me something to wear!'

He was in the process of phoning Ryan before they left the ambulance to explain what had happened, and went on to tell him that he was going to the apartment to get cleaned up before going to the hospital, but would be there with all speed as the emergency, which on the face of it was neurological, could have orthopaedic problems as well.

'And so how is Leonie, the heroine of the hour?' his friend asked.

'Cold and exhausted,' was the reply, 'and looks as if she might be developing a fever. I'm taking her where I can keep an eye on her and will be in touch again soon.'

They were in the apartment, wet and bedraggled, with Leonie's blanket trailing behind her. It might have seemed comical in other circumstances, Callum thought grimly, but not tonight.

The boy, Midge, could have drowned out there if she hadn't swum out to him and so could she. The water was unbelievably deep at the other side of the weir and if he had lost her he would have gone insane.

The moment they were inside Leonie had sunk down onto a chair, and aware of the state she was in he went to run a bath for her immediately and left a robe and pyjamas near for her to put on when she'd had a long warm soak.

'I don't need those things,' she told him weakly. 'I'm coming with you.'

'No way!' he told her. 'I've made you a warm drink and as soon as you are out of the bath it must be into bed in the master bedroom at the front of the building.'

'And where will you sleep when you come back?'

His smile was wry. 'No need to panic. I'll be in the guest room.' He frowned. 'I wish I didn't have to leave you in this state, feverish and exhausted.'

'Just go and see to the boy,' she said softly. 'I'll be fine.'

'All right,' he agreed. 'As soon as I've whizzed in and out of the shower I'll be off. And, Leonie, make sure you have your phone handy while I'm gone.'

CHAPTER EIGHT

WHEN HE ARRIVED at the hospital the first boy was waiting for his parents to arrive, having been cleaned up, found dry clothing, and in the meantime was enjoying his brief moment of notoriety, until his father arrived and told him off big time for sneaking out of the house to do something so dangerous.

Callum had gone straight to Theatre and when he and Ryan reappeared they had to tell Midge's parents that he had a deep head wound that was being scanned before they made any diagnosis.

'What about the nurse who rescued our son?' his mother asked anxiously into the silence that had fallen on the waiting room. 'Is *she* all right?'

'Er, Leonie Mitchell is not too well at the

moment due to the after-effects of what happened,' he told them, 'but is most concerned about your son.'

'You can go to him while we're waiting for the result,' Ryan told the parents. 'He has regained consciousness and is talking normally to the nurses who are with him, and as soon as we have news for you we'll be back.'

As they proceeded to the ward Ryan said, 'Callum, why don't you go and see to Leonie? We've not found any broken bones or suchlike that require your expertise. The problems will be with the skull, which is my department, and I can always give you a buzz if necessary.'

'Yes, OK,' Callum agreed gratefully. 'I left her having a bath and am keen to know that she managed it and is now warm and comfortable after what happened, though knowing Leonie she won't have settled until she knows how the boy is.' He turned to go. 'How is Melissa? Any sign of my godson yet?'

'No, not yet,' he was told. 'If he's on time it should be next week.'

'Melissa said you folks would like Leonie to be godmother—has she asked her yet?'

'No, but she's going to when she gets around to it.'

'Fine!' Callum said, and off he went, hoping that Leonie might have changed her mind and would feel the same about it as he did.

When he arrived back at the apartment he called her name the second he was through the door but there was no answer, and having checked that she wasn't in any of the downstairs rooms thought thankfully that she must have done as he'd said and gone straight to bed after the bath.

But the bedroom door wasn't closed, as he would have expected it to be, and when he reached the landing he saw her lying face down on the carpet dressed in his pyjamas, with no sound or movement to be heard or seen. He was beside her in a flash.

He turned her over gently and saw that she was pale and puffy faced. He felt her pulse and it was erratic, so was her heartbeat, and when Leonie opened her eyes and observed him it was as if she was looking at a stranger. She began to cry and call out for someone called Benedict. The guy from her past that she would never talk about?

She kept on calling for him and he decided it must have been some affair that the two of them had been engaged in for her to be crying for him like this, which was a dampening thought as far as he was concerned. It was no wonder that she was keeping him at a distance if she was still carrying the torch for this fellow.

On impulse he went into the bathroom and tested the bathwater that was still there. It was quite hot, which was surprising as he'd been away for an hour or more. Had she immersed herself in water that was too hot in her chilled state?

It wasn't something Leonie would do normally but she hadn't been normal when he'd left her, had she? She'd been chilled to the bone, and all medical folk and lots of others too knew that to bring heat to the body of someone dangerously cold could do more harm than good if it was done too hot and too fast, that they must be warmed gradually until back to normal.

When she called for Benedict again he winced at the sound but told her gently that he would try to bring him to her, and wondered if Julie would be able to tell him how to find this guy that he would like to throttle for causing Leonie to be so distraught.

For a second Leonie was lucid, observing him in bewilderment and crying, 'You can't!' As she turned her face into the pillow he wondered what that was supposed to mean.

She had closed her eyes again and he checked

her temperature, heartbeat, pulse and blood pressure once more. To his relief there was a slight improvement.

When he looked at Leonie she seemed to be sleeping naturally and he went downstairs to make a drink. He drew back the curtains and it was incredible to find that it was barely daylight after not the best night in either of their lives.

First he'd experienced the horror of seeing her swimming in the deepest part of the river in just a nightdress, followed by her loss of body heat, which had really worried him, and then, fool that he was, in his concern for the boy he'd left Leonie, who'd been anything but well, to have a bath when she had been on the border of hypothermia. It would seem that somehow she had thawed out too quickly for whatever reason and made herself really ill.

Also, bordering on delirium, she had wept for someone called Benedict to come to her, yet when he'd offered to try to locate him she'd said he couldn't.

But a positive of all that had happened was that he'd been there for her when she'd needed him most…or had he? Had he been ready to put the job first?

As he looked out unseeingly at the morning that was unfolding itself out of the darkness of the night Ryan was getting out of his car on the forecourt of the apartments and Callum hastened to let him in.

'Thought I'd call to see how your patient is and to report on mine,' he said as Callum passed him a coffee from the pot.

'Leonie is not good,' Callum told him sombrely. 'I came back to find her out of it on the bedroom floor and when she came round she was delirious, calling all the time for some guy that she's pining for.

'I've been doing all the usual checks on her and she's improved slightly, is sleeping naturally, but I have a feeling that she was on the verge of hypothermia when I left her and might have warmed herself up too quickly in the bath, because she was confused, managed to get out and get dressed then collapsed. I was a fool to have left her.

'And now tell me about Midge. What's the score with him? It will be the first thing Leonie asks when she's fully recovered.'

'Fractured skull, no brain damage thankfully, or bone fragments. We've done the necessary and he should be all right eventually.'

'That's good—two serious situations, two hopeful recoveries.'

Ryan was getting up wearily from the chair that he'd perched himself on. 'I need to get back to Melissa and the girls,' he said. 'With the baby so near I don't want to be far away from them, but I had to find out how Leonie was. Now I'll be able to report back to those at home and get some sleep.'

When he'd gone Callum went back upstairs and found Leonie sitting up against the pillows, still pale and puffy-looking but with her gaze clear of any confusion, and when she smiled at him his heart leapt with thankfulness.

'So tell me what happened,' he said softly.

'I was so cold that I couldn't wait to warm myself in the bath,' she told him, 'and heated up the water because it didn't seem hot enough. When I got in it felt lovely, but within minutes I didn't know what I was doing. I felt so ill, I was confused, but knew vaguely that I had to get out of the bath and just managed to do that and put the pyjamas on before everything went black. Obviously I had hypothermia but was too ill to realise it.'

'And how do you feel now?' he asked. 'I can't believe that I left you in that state. Do forgive me, Leonie.'

'You did nothing wrong, Callum. I was all right when you went. What happened to me was partly self-inflicted. How long was it before I regained consciousness when you found me?'

'Not long, but you were delirious for a while afterwards and kept asking for someone called Benedict, whoever he might be.'

He watched bright colour stain the puffiness of her face and hoped for an explanation, but there was none forthcoming, just a weak smile and a shrug of the shoulders inside his voluminous pyjamas.

In that moment he gave up on a love that he knew was hopeless as far as he was concerned, unaware that he had just rendered her speechless from discovering that the ache that she carried around with her had surfaced in front of Callum.

It was obvious what he was thinking and the truth would take only seconds to clear the air, but what the two of *them* had was clean and beautiful. Did she want to spoil it?

'I feel well enough to go home now if you

wouldn't mind taking me,' she said quickly. 'Thank you for looking after me. I needed a friend and you were there, as I knew you would be.'

She brushed her hand gently across his cheek and smiling down at her he asked, 'Is a friend allowed to do this?'

He kissed her tenderly then went to find his car keys and a wrap of some sort to cover the pyjamas.

It took only a matter of minutes and they were outside the yurt that she had left the night before for what had been intended to be a breath of air to relieve her sleeplessness, and as Callum came round to her side of the car to help her out he said, 'As this place has been unlocked all night I'll come in with you for a second to make sure that everything is all right inside.'

Leonie nodded mutely. She could still feel his kiss bringing her senses to life and increasing the longing for him that she lived with day and night, but her secrecy had gone too far this time. She'd been crying for a child that he'd thought was an adult, and he had been willing to go in search of him for her.

All was as she'd left it in the yurt and after a quick glance around he was ready to go, but he paused for a moment to say, 'Take some time off to recover from last night, and if you have any more after-effects send for me.'

It was on the tip of her tongue to tell him that she was already suffering from after-effects, but they were from bringing the not-so-far-away past into the open. Callum deserved an explanation and she watched him drive away with a lump in her throat.

Leonie was sitting in the sun outside the yurt in the early afternoon, deep in thought, when Julie turned up, having only just heard about the river episode from someone at the community centre.

'You are something else!' she said, giving her a hug. 'And Callum was involved too I'm told. I guess you didn't complain about that?'

'True,' Leonie admitted. 'I didn't complain at all, at first! It was magical when he appeared beside me in the river. Together we got the boy to the bank and managed to get the water out of his lungs.

'Then when an ambulance arrived Callum sent him to the hospital and asked Ryan Ferguson to go there to treat him, as he had a bad head wound, while the two of us went to the apartment to get cleaned up and warm. I was absolutely frozen and it was then that it all went wrong.'

'How?'

'I'd got a touch of hypothermia, became confused and kept crying out for Benedict. When I was rational again Callum asked me who he was and I couldn't get the words out to tell him.

The result being that he now thinks that Benedict is a lover.'

'Oh, no!' Julie exclaimed. 'Callum Warrender is the catch of Heatherdale and he wants you, for goodness' sake! You aren't treating him fairly.

'I know how you feel about the past and can understand your reluctance to talk about it because the pain of it is always there, but, Leonie, for heaven's sake, you did nothing wrong. You were a victim, not a culprit.'

'Yes, but I should have known what I was letting myself in for with Adrian,' she said. 'Finding out he was married was horrendous, but nothing will ever hurt as much as losing my baby.'

'No, of course not,' Julie agreed sympathetically, 'and it is your life. What you can live with in peace is all that matters.'

When Julie had gone the day seemed never-ending in the quietness of the yurt. Callum rang briefly to make sure that she was continuing to improve from the trauma of the night, and just the sound of his voice was enough to lift her spirits, even though she felt it was more of a duty call than anything else.

'I'm all right,' she told him. 'Improving by the minute.'

'So what have you been doing since I left you? Nothing strenuous, I hope?'

'No, of course not. Julie came round and gave me a telling-off about a few things and for the rest of the time I've been resting.'

'Your best friend told you off? That seems strange.'

'Yes, well, I suppose I've been asking for it,' she said flatly, and was relieved when he didn't pursue the subject because he had a message to deliver.

'Melissa has been on to me about you,' he told her. 'She's concerned about you being so unwell after being in the river and has asked me to bring her to see you tonight. Obviously I said yes, that we would call in at about seven. Be prepared, Leonie, she is going to mention the christening.'

'All right, thanks for the warning,' she told him levelly. 'And just one thing more before you ring off. The boy, Midge, how is he?'

'Bouncing back, mentally and physically. Got a sore head that could have been a lot worse if Ryan hadn't come out to him in the middle of the night. And by the way, everyone on the wards sends their good wishes and hopes that you'll soon be back with us. Now I must go, I'm due in Theatre.'

When he came with Melissa in the evening Callum wasn't relishing being present when Leonie refused to be the baby's godmother. But she must have her reasons, he told himself, because she loved being with children of all ages and it was going to be completely out of character.

The three of them had chatted for a while before Melissa brought up the subject and he felt his jaw go slack when Leonie said, 'I would love to be godmother to your and Ryan's baby, Melissa. It will be a privilege and a delight.'

They didn't stay long as Melissa was heavy with the last few days of pregnancy and Callum was keen not to overtire Leonie after the scare with the bath water. So there was no opportunity to ask why the change of mind, but it would be the first thing he mentioned the next time they spoke, which might be in a few days if she took some time off as he'd told her to.

How much notice she had taken of that became evident when he saw her cycling along in front of him the next morning, hospital bound, and when they met in the car park she spoke before he had the chance and told him, 'I know you said not to be too quick to get back into routine, Callum, but I feel fine now, and haven't forgotten that I wasn't the only one who was wet through, and *you* had to rush to the hospital within seconds of having arrived at the apartment with barely time to get dried or have a hot drink. So here I am, desperate to be back where you are.'

He observed her thoughtfully. 'Are you quite sure about that? It isn't a follow-on to your change of heart regarding being the baby's godmother? That for once you are relaxing the rules that you live by?'

'No, nothing like that, and any rules that I live by are not of my choosing,' she told him, and went to put the bike away without a backward glance. She made her way to the unit to start the day, with the pleasure of being close to Callum again disappearing like water down a drain.

They did the ward rounds together, like they always did, and as they moved from bed to bed Callum said of a pale-faced little girl who was sitting up in bed and holding her mother's hand tightly, 'This is Joely, she was admitted yesterday when you were not with us, and has a funny hip that keeps clicking out of place. I'm hoping to put that right in Theatre this afternoon.'

At that moment the phone in the ward office rang and he went to answer it. She heard him say, 'Wonderful! And are mother and baby all right?' After a pause while his question was answered he said, 'Yes, I'll tell her. Leonie is here and will be just as delighted as I am to hear that all is well.'

She was smiling her relief as he said, 'I don't need to tell you what that was about, do I?'

'No,' she breathed. 'Melissa has had the baby and they are both fine. It must be a great relief after the accident when it could have been so different, and I'm so happy for her and Ryan that they will be bringing their new little one into a loving, carefree home.'

Her voice had thickened with emotion. On impulse he said casually, 'What sort of a family was yours?'

'All right, I suppose,' she told him, 'except I would have liked some brothers and sisters, but my mother had a top job in the city, and my father, who had a pilot's licence as I once explained, was obsessed with flying, and it was through that I lost them. I suppose I was happy enough until then but afterwards was lost and lonely.'

'I wish I'd been around at that time,' he said gently.

'Yes, I wish you had been too, *you have no idea how much*!' she said, and it was as if that was as far as she was going to go regarding her life before they'd met, as she'd turned her attention to the small apprehensive girl and mother with her usual caring approach.

As one part of Callum's mind was taking in what she was saying, the rest of it was experiencing the feeling of having been on the brink of hearing something that he desperately needed to know, but if his past success rate when he'd tried to coax Leonie to talk about herself was anything to go by, it could be a long time coming.

Summer had come to Heatherdale. The hills and dales were wearing the rich green mantle of the time of year, and the parks in the famous small market town were ablaze with flowers and ancient trees in full leaf that added to its delights.

With summer came the tourists to this place that had a charm all of its own, and Leonie wondered if she and Callum would ever go on the sightseeing tour that he had suggested, as their relationship felt as if it had been put on hold ever since the night when she'd cried out for her baby and left him totally uninformed as to who Benedict was or had been.

Their working relationship at the hospital was still the same, but he never came to call at the yurt or asked her out, and she had to console herself with the thought that at least they would be together socially at the christening, which was to take place in two weeks' time.

The difference in their lives at present was that he had two special events to look forward to—the visit of his mother and stepfather in the near future and the christening—and she had none.

She viewed the baptism as an ordeal where she was going to be affected by the atmosphere and the words she would have to say, and with regard to the visit of his parents she had no joy of that kind to look forward to because she didn't have her own.

The christening was to take place in an old stone church near to where Melissa and Ryan lived and where his first wife was buried, with the grave of Melissa's grandmother close by, and on the Friday before the Sunday when it was to take place, as they were leaving the hospital, Callum said, 'Are you sure you will be all right for the ceremony?'

'Yes,' she told him, 'I would never do anything to upset Ryan and Melissa.'

'Of course not. So I'll call for you on Sunday morning. I need your advice on what kind
of a gift to take. What is the usual thing for a
christening?'

'There are a few, such as a little silver casket
for the baby's first tooth or a lock of its hair.
Some godparents open a savings account for it.'

'That sounds more like my type of thing. I'll
sort it tomorrow.'

'I've got a special baby book for Melissa and
Ryan to record his progress all through childhood, with lots of lovely pictures in it too,' she
told him.

'Sounds as if you've given more thought to it
than I have,' he said ruefully.

'Maybe that is because I've had more time
than you to shop around,' she said, smiling
across at him, but he had no smile for her in
return, just the thought that being busy helped

to deal with his disappointment regarding what was happening to their relationship, and how would she feel if he carried her off to some remote island where she could put her dark thoughts to one side and let him make love to her instead of being on the edge of her life?

Before she had the chance to reply to the implied rebuke he left, asking himself the question that he always did on this sort of occasion. *Was he ever going to be able to leave Leonie with joy in his heart after one of their meetings?*

The only time she'd given him hope that she felt as he did had been on the night when he'd followed her from the hotel and questioned if it was because she'd wanted to get away from him.

She'd told him it was the opposite, that she'd gone because she had been desperate to look upon him, if only for a moment, but once she'd seen him she'd panicked and left the place.

Yet even then he had felt no chemistry on her

part, just a tender farewell, and when the door had closed behind her he'd gone home foolishly content.

When he called for Leonie on the morning of the christening she was wearing a cream dress and a wide-brimmed hat of black straw that shadowed the green eyes beneath it to some extent, and made him want to tilt it back to look into them, but she was already walking out to the car and they needed to get to the church in time.

Ryan and his family were well known in Heatherdale and the church was full of well-wishers and members of the opposite sex who would have liked to be his second wife but hadn't stood a chance from the moment he'd met Melissa on a cold, dark winter night.

The christening party was at the front with Rhianna and Martha seated between Leonie and Callum until the moment that the baptism was to take place, and each time Callum glanced across at Leonie he was aware of her attempt to avoid eye contact by means of the hat, but why, for heaven's sake?

She couldn't be too reluctant to take part, having changed her mind from her original decision, but the hand holding on to her order of service was clutching it so tightly that her knuckles were showing white. If the children hadn't been sitting between them he would have taken her hand in his and stroked it gently.

When it was Leonie's turn to make her responses during the baptism she was calmer than she would ever have believed possible, but each time she looked down at the baby's face as she held him in her arms, the longing and the pain that never went away was there, and although her hold of the little one was safe and steady the colour was draining from her face.

Callum, who had never taken his glance off her, placed his arm around her and said softly,

'You are doing fine. We both are.' Looking down on to the baby, he said, 'I can give you one of these if you'll let me. I don't give a damn about what it is that holds you back from admitting that you love me. I know you, and in knowing you can't believe you would ever do anything that you have to keep bottled up so tightly.'

The colour was coming back to her face, her world was righting itself for a short space of time, and during the rest of the christening she did what she was there to do without faltering or fuss. And when along with other guests they went back to Ryan and Melissa's house, where a buffet was waiting for them, Leonie was weak with the relief of not having spoilt the ceremony with her sad memories.

She had Callum to thank for that. Could it be that he'd guessed from where they came?

She could see him in the garden, holding the baby with the children playing close by, and went out to join them, and as if he sensed her watching him he looked up and smiled. When she went to sit beside him he said whimsically, 'Can we have the hat off now that the ordeal is over? I'm not happy if I can't see your eyes. You will remember my offer, I hope.'

'It will be engraved upon my heart,' she told him lightly, though nothing had changed. The fact that she'd survived the christening without spoiling it for everyone didn't mean that she wasn't still afraid to face another commitment, even with Callum.

CHAPTER NINE

'I'M GOING TO go when I've made my excuses to Melissa and Ryan,' she said, following on that downbeat thought, and he frowned.

'Why exactly?'

'I need to speak to Julie about something.'

'Can't it wait?'

'Er, no, not really.'

'Do you want me to drive you there?' He looked down at the infant that he was still holding. 'I'll give Liam to his mother and come back when I've taken you, as I would hate to think that both his godparents had left so soon.'

Ignoring the last part of his comment, she told him, 'I don't need a lift. I intend to walk there. It's only a short distance away, but thanks just the same.' She went to make her apologies for leaving early.

What she'd said to Callum had been true. She did need to speak to Julie, though the need to do so urgently had only just surfaced when she'd told him, and she knew he hadn't been pleased, but suddenly to talk to the only person who knew what had happened to her was vital and she had to do it immediately.

'I'm going to tell Callum what he wants to know,' she said when she arrived at the small studio flat that was Julie's and Brendan's home for the time being.

'Really!' she exclaimed. 'So why the change of heart?'

'I can't go on the way I have been with Callum. He deserves better than that. He was so kind to me at the christening because he knew that I was dreading it for some reason, but didn't know why, and I've left him looking down on the baby like the wonderful father he would be for a child of his own.

'*His* life is all mapped out for him in this lovely place. He has his position at the hospital, his friends and colleagues, and a reputation second to none, while I've always felt like a passing ship, but I don't any longer, Julie.

'When we first met he was set on giving marriage and all that went with it a wide berth, even to forgoing the family that he had longed for, but now he's put all that to one side and wants us to have children of our own, which I long for too. Although amongst the uncertainties that I live with is the dread that I might have another stillbirth, and he needs to be told about that.'

'Don't concern yourself too much over that,' her friend said gently. 'The guy loves *you* first and foremost, and that is all that matters. You are so right for each other, Leonie. So when are you going to tell him?'

'The first chance I get,' she said, with some new determination strong within in her.

She didn't stay at Julie's long. It was Sunday night and she would be back on the wards tomorrow, waiting for the right opportunity for them to talk, when she would tell Callum what she had kept from him. So once Julie had expressed her joy and relief at the news she had brought, Leonie went home to await the morning.

She was on the unit, discussing with other nursing staff the treatment that Callum had arranged when he'd been called out late after the christening to a young girl who had been at a birthday party that seemed to have got out of hand and had sustained a serious neck injury, and now he was back on the job and telling her in a low voice, 'You missed a great occasion by rushing off like that. It must have been very urgent.'

'It was,' she told him, and in her haste to create a better understanding between them, said, 'Would it be convenient for you to show me round the town and the surrounding country-side some time this coming weekend?'

She was expecting him to say yes and was disappointed when he shook his head and said, 'I can't, I'm afraid. That's when my mother and stepfather are arriving for a two-week visit and I will be fully occupied. Would you like to come round for a meal so that you can meet them in-stead?'

'Yes, I would love to,' she told him. With some of her determination of the night before dwindling, it would be an occasion to look back on in times to come if he wasn't impressed by what she had to tell him.

'I won't be at the hospital much while they're here,' he said. 'The same doctor who filled in for me when I was at the seminar will do so again, so I might have to phone you to agree on an evening for you to join us. Are you likely to be free?

'Yes, of course,' she told him, and wondered what he thought she did at night apart from visiting the community centre sometimes.

Meeting Callum's mother and stepfather would be an opportunity for them to be together in the vacuum that his family's visit was going to cause over the next two weeks, but it would provide no opportunity for the kind of thing she was going to tell him, and after being unwilling for so long now she really did want to wipe the slate clean, and for the rest of the week she was on edge.

Callum was aware of her anxiety, the same as he was aware of everything about her, but as no reason was given when he questioned it he gave up and concentrated on the pleasure to come of seeing his mother and the amiable Brent in Heatherdale for a short space of time.

He'd been surprised when Leonie had wanted

to meet them, would have thought she would see it as further entanglement with him in her life, but it had seemed that she would be only too pleased to meet his family. For him it would be happiness untold to have the two women that he loved totally getting to know each other, in spite of the fact that the best ward sister he'd ever worked with continued to keep him at a distance.

The coming weekend when Callum would be involved with his visitors was going to be long and empty, Leonie thought, even if she went to the community centre on both nights, but consoled herself with the thought that there was the meeting with his parents to compensate and, anxious as she was to open her heart to him, she was not going to do it before that.

So when there was a shortage of staff over the weekend she volunteered, as she sometimes did, not expecting him to call at the yurt on Sunday afternoon to arrange the proposed meeting with his parents while they were sleeping off jet-lag.

Callum was disappointed not to find her there but thought wryly that knowing Leonie she wouldn't be sitting around, meekly awaiting his commands. So he pushed a note under the door to ask if Tuesday night would be all right for her to join them and that he would come for her if it was.

When she came home and saw it she groaned at the thought of not having been there when he'd come. Every moment spent with him was precious.

She rang him when she'd stopped fretting about it and said, 'Can you guess where I was when you came?'

'Am I likely to?' he wanted to know.

'It's a place that you see a lot of.'

'Not the hospital, by any chance?'

'Yes, they were short-staffed over the weekend, so having nothing else to do I volunteered.

Tuesday will suit me fine, Callum. There's no need to come for me, I can walk to your place in a matter of minutes.'

'Yes, well, we'll see about that on the night,' he said. 'What would you prefer, that the four of us dine in one of the hotels in the town, or that I cook for us?'

'A hotel,' she told him. 'If you cook you'll be in the kitchen all the time, and I don't know your parents and they don't know me.'

'All right, hotel it is,' he agreed. 'Now I must go. I hear voices, which would seem to mean that my mother and Brent have surfaced after sleeping off the effects of the flight.

'Take care, Leonie, don't do anything rash before I see you again.'

Callum rang again briefly on Monday to say he'd made a reservation at the hotel where Julian's wedding reception had taken place and would call for her and take her to the apartment to meet his parents before they left for the town centre.

It had been a hot and sultry day and the unit had been even busier than usual without him. Detecting a flatness about her voice, he asked, 'What's wrong, Leonie? You are not going to let me down on this, I hope?'

'No, of course not,' she told him. 'I'm just tired, that's all, but am really looking forward to tomorrow night.'

She was wearing the green dress that matched her eyes when Callum called for her the following night, and she presented a calm that belied her inward nervousness at the prospect of what she had blithely thought was a good idea and now wasn't so sure about. But there was no way that Callum was going to know that, and when they arrived at his apartment and he introduced her to his parents she had her doubts under control.

From his mother Margaret's point of view she was observing the kind of woman that she would love to have as a daughter-in-law, if only Callum would open up and tell her how much this person meant to him, because the fact that he had invited her to meet them had to mean something.

She had stood by helplessly when he'd married Shelley and couldn't bear the thought of another fiasco like that had been, but she sensed that this was different and hope was kindling.

The evening was a huge success for all of them, with Leonie forgetting what the future held for a while, Callum aware of his mother's approval of the love of his life, and his stepfather beaming good-naturedly upon them.

When they stopped outside the yurt at the end of the evening he said, 'Mum and Brent are going to Manchester for the day on Saturday so I will be free to show you the delights of Heatherdale after all, if you wish.'

'Yes, if you can spare the time,' she told him, as the magic of the last few hours faded at the thought of what lay ahead, but it would be the right time to tell him what she had to tell without another week of thinking about it.

'It has been lovely to meet you,' Margaret told her as they said their goodbyes, holding close for a moment the woman whose sad eyes belied her bright smile.

Tears pricked Leonie's eyes at the thought of what it would be like to have this woman as well as Callum in her life.

After seeing her safely inside, they went and Saturday loomed up for her like doomsday.

The weather on the day was how she felt, Leonie thought when she drew back the curtains—dark and miserable with no sun in the sky. It was raining, a heavy drizzle, but she didn't want them to cancel their time together and hoped that Callum was feeling the same.

It seemed that he was. He rang to say that if she was still interested so was he, and maybe they should start the scenic tour in the town and then work their way upwards if and when the rain stopped, and not to bother with food as they would most likely be near somewhere to eat around lunchtime.

When he'd hung up Leonie wished that it really was a sightseeing excursion instead of confession time, but hadn't changed her mind, and so she dressed in jeans, a cotton top and walking shoes and waited for him to appear.

'Why do I have a feeling that you are not looking forward to this?' Callum asked when she opened to door to him.

'You are wrong,' she told him, and thought if she had never told a lie before, that one would make up for all the others and changed the subject. 'I loved everything about your mother, Callum. She is delightful.'

'Yes, she is,' he agreed. 'Her greatest wish is

to see me married to someone I adore and that the two of us give her grandchildren. How are you fixed, Leonie? You know how I feel, but I can't say that I get to know much about your side of things as you keep me on a knife edge where that's concerned.'

'Not any more,' she said in a low voice. 'I asked for this day with you to tell you the truth about me that I have been too afraid to bring out in the open...or I suppose it might be that deceit becomes me.'

'Hardly.'

'Oh, yes! I had an affair with someone at the London hospital where I worked, and not only did he make me pregnant but I had no idea that he was married until I was confronted by his wife on his behalf and was told that he'd done the kind of thing he did to me before and had no intention of leaving her. She even suggested that if I didn't want the baby, they would take it.

'You've seen me with children, Callum, and

there was no way that he was even going to get near it, but my baby, my beautiful baby, was stillborn at full term, and it was then that Julie came on the scene and helped me to face up to my loss.

'I know that I behaved with incredible stupidity to let that man into my life, but I'd just lost my parents and was so lonely and griefstricken that I let him use me, expecting that we would get married once the baby was born, but it was all lies.'

Callum's face was darkening, his mouth tightening, but he hadn't said a word while she'd been speaking, and she said finally, 'I know it doesn't make nice telling.'

'So Benedict was your baby?' he said, ignoring her last comment.

'Yes.'

'I was jealous as hell, thought he was a lover or something of the sort.'

'And yet you offered to try and find him and bring him to me.'

'Yes. It was the least I could do. Leonie, what makes you so sure that I won't understand? I come from a family where there was love all around me, the love of a woman for a child born outside marriage—*me*.

'You met her the other night. My mother worked ceaselessly to give me all the things that I might have missed being fatherless, and made sure I never felt abandoned or different from my friends, or cheated of the kind of things that other kids had. And I know you would have been the same when something very similar to what happened to her happened to you.'

He held out his arms and as she went into them like a nesting bird, he said gently, 'So do you feel better after that? I'm not going to give up on you.'

'I don't want you to, Callum, I love you so much,' she whispered.

'So can we begin to arrange wedding number three? But first, before anything else, can I phone my mother to tell her that her wishes have been granted?'

'Yes, of course,' she said, glowing up at him. 'I can't believe I'm going to have a family again as well as a fantastic husband.'

It was the middle of the afternoon, after they'd lunched in the town with champagne laid on, when Callum suggested that they walk up to the moors and leave the sightseeing until another time, and it wasn't long before they came to the bend in the road where they had first met, and perched on the stone wall.

'We have been here so many joyless times,' he said, 'that I think it is only fitting that we come on one of the happiest days of our lives, don't you?'

'Yes, oh, yes!' she agreed.

'So can I put this on your finger?' he asked

gravely, 'so that you don't forget that you are going to marry me?' He produced the emerald ring that he had thought he would never see in its rightful place and went on to say, 'I chose it because it is the same colour as your eyes.' As he slipped it on he said, 'How soon do you think we can have the church bells ringing for *us*?'

They'd bought a gracious Victorian house beside the river with the completion of the sale in eight weeks' time, and so had arranged the wedding to coincide with that.

Margaret had been overcome with delight to hear their news and she and Brent would be paying a second visit to Heatherdale for the occasion, needless to say.

Rhianna and Martha were to be bridesmaids, along with Julie, and Ryan was to be best man, while the staff on the orthopaedic unit was drawing lots for who should get time off to attend, as poorly children had to come first. For those who couldn't be there, cake and champagne would be sent round from the reception.

They'd given Yoris the yurt to Julie and Brendan to save them having to pay rent on the flat, and everything was organised for the big day that Leonie had thought she would never see.

Even the weather was perfect when she opened the curtains in the yurt for the last time, as they were still living separately at Callum's insistence because he wanted to do things properly for Leonie.

The sun was high in the sky, birds were chirping, ducks on the river were swimming their graceful way along its waters, *and it was her wedding day. She had never been so happy in her life!*

Callum was waiting for her at the altar, the man she would love and cherish for the rest of her life, and as she walked up the aisle, holding the arm of his stepfather, wearing a wedding dress of cream brocade with her veil floating behind and carrying a bouquet of red roses, her dream was coming true.

Callum turned, and it was there in the dark hazel of his eyes, the promise that she would never be alone again, that he would cherish her always.

EPILOGUE

IT WAS SPRING again, time for new life to appear, and Leonie and Callum Warrender were looking forward to the arrival of some new life of their own in the maternity unit of a large hospital not far away.

She was in labour, with contractions coming fast and with fear in her heart for the baby girl that they had created together. She'd been assured that her baby was perfectly healthy and there was no cause for alarm, but those who were telling her that hadn't been around when Benedict had been delivered, small, still and lifeless.

Only Callum understood her fears and he was right there beside her, checking the baby's heartbeat and assuring her that it was fine. But it wouldn't be until she held their daughter in her arms and heard her cry that Leonie would be able to rejoice.

He bent to check it again and she said urgently, 'She's coming, Callum, our daughter. Please don't let anything happen to her!'

'I won't,' he promised, and a few seconds later the lusty cry of a newborn was heard and Leonie wept tears of joy at the sound. She held out her arms, and as he placed their child in them he said, 'I wonder if Benedict knows he's got a little sister?'

'I am sure he does,' she said softly, and in the next breath, 'I really do love you, Callum.'

'And I love you, my beautiful wife,' he told her. 'You are the centre of my existence and always will be.'

* * * * *

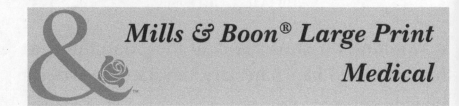

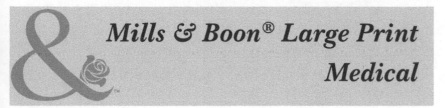

Mills & Boon® Large Print
Medical

March

A SECRET SHARED...	Marion Lennox
FLIRTING WITH THE DOC OF HER DREAMS	Janice Lynn
THE DOCTOR WHO MADE HER LOVE AGAIN	Susan Carlisle
THE MAVERICK WHO RULED HER HEART	Susan Carlisle
AFTER ONE FORBIDDEN NIGHT...	Amber McKenzie
DR PERFECT ON HER DOORSTEP	Lucy Clark

April

IT STARTED WITH NO STRINGS...	Kate Hardy
ONE MORE NIGHT WITH HER DESERT PRINCE...	Jennifer Taylor
FLIRTING WITH DR OFF-LIMITS	Robin Gianna
FROM FLING TO FOREVER	Avril Tremayne
DARE SHE DATE AGAIN?	Amy Ruttan
THE SURGEON'S CHRISTMAS WISH	Annie O'Neil

May

PLAYING THE PLAYBOY'S SWEETHEART	Carol Marinelli
UNWRAPPING HER ITALIAN DOC	Carol Marinelli
A DOCTOR BY DAY...	Emily Forbes
TAMED BY THE RENEGADE	Emily Forbes
A LITTLE CHRISTMAS MAGIC	Alison Roberts
CHRISTMAS WITH THE MAVERICK	Scarlet Wilson